The Quotable Anaïs Nin

Volume Two

THE QUOTABLE ANAÏS NIN

365 Quotations with Citations

Volume Two

Collected and compiled by

Paul Herron

With engravings by Ian Hugo

Sky Blue Press
State College, Pennsylvania

Published by Sky Blue Press, State College, Pennsylvania

ISBN: 978-1-7357459-1-6
Library of Congress Control Number: 2015954907

eBook ISBN: 978-1-7357459-2-3

Special thanks to:

The Anaïs Nin Trust

TABLE OF CONTENTS

INTRODUCTION

The work of Anaïs Nin (1903-1977), as the first volume of this series demonstrates, is the source of many quotations that seem to speak to us today as strongly as the day they were published in her diaries, fiction, and used in her lectures and interviews. One recognizes their popularity when one googles "Anaïs Nin quotes": nearly 2,000,000 results appear.

The internet, while an important and handy source of information, can be a source of misinformation. Quotations have been misattributed to Nin, most famously the "Risk" poem. Sometimes Nin's words are misquoted, or cited incorrectly if at all.

Both volumes of *The Quotable Anaïs Nin* present quotations exactly as they appear in print and cite their sources. A general rule is that the quotation's citation indicates the *original* source. Nin's publication history is rather complicated: for example, about half of the first volume of *The Diary of Anaïs Nin* (published in 1966) and the "unexpurgated" *Henry & June* (1986) cover the same time period (1931-1932); sometimes passages are used in both books for the sake of context and storyline. Any such quotation would be cited from the *Diary* because it was published first. If the *Henry & June* quotation is significantly different than the one in the *Diary*, and has been deemed by this editor to be superior, then the *Henry & June* version is used. This is true of all the expurgated and unexpurgated diaries, and Nin's fiction when more than one version was published.

An exception to the rule is Nin's *roman fleuve*, consisting of five novels, each of which appeared individually at some point, in various editions by various publishers, but were finally collected in an omnibus volume, *Cities of the Interior*, the final form of which was published in 1961 by Swallow Press. For the sake of simplicity, quotations from any of these novels are cited from *Cities*.

A second exception is the quotations that appear in *Conversations with Anaïs Nin*, which are collected from other sources. For the sake of simplicity, we cite the collection itself and not the individual original sources.

Several quotations appear here from as-yet-unpublished works, most notably the final two unexpurgated diaries; since these books have yet to be formatted in a final form, instead of using page numbers for citation, the year a quotation was written is provided.

The contents of *The Quotable Anaïs Nin* are divided into general themes that reflect the characteristics of Nin's writing: lust for life, love and sensuality, consciousness, women and men, and writing and art. Unlike the first volume of *The Quotable Anaïs Nin*, the quotations here are very loosely arranged in a way that follows a theme-based thread.

Both volumes of *The Quotable Anaïs Nin* can be used for inspiration and for reference. The reason 365 quotations are presented here is so that there is literally a quotation for each day of the year.

Of course, it is my hope that the reader will be inspired to investigate the sources from which favorite quotations come; to read them in context of the complete work is a meaningful and satisfying endeavor.

—Paul Herron, March 2021

a way of escaping tragedy. What I have often regretted is having given John that first élan, knowing each time the élan would lose a little in vigor -- and Allendy has received the easiest, the most moderate of all!

I hate to feel that my incapacity to face the greatest pains of love is making me afraid of absolutism. It is true I had no fear of my absolute love for Henry, yet even then I was counting on Allendy's paternal care of me and I turned towards him the day June returned — during my panic.

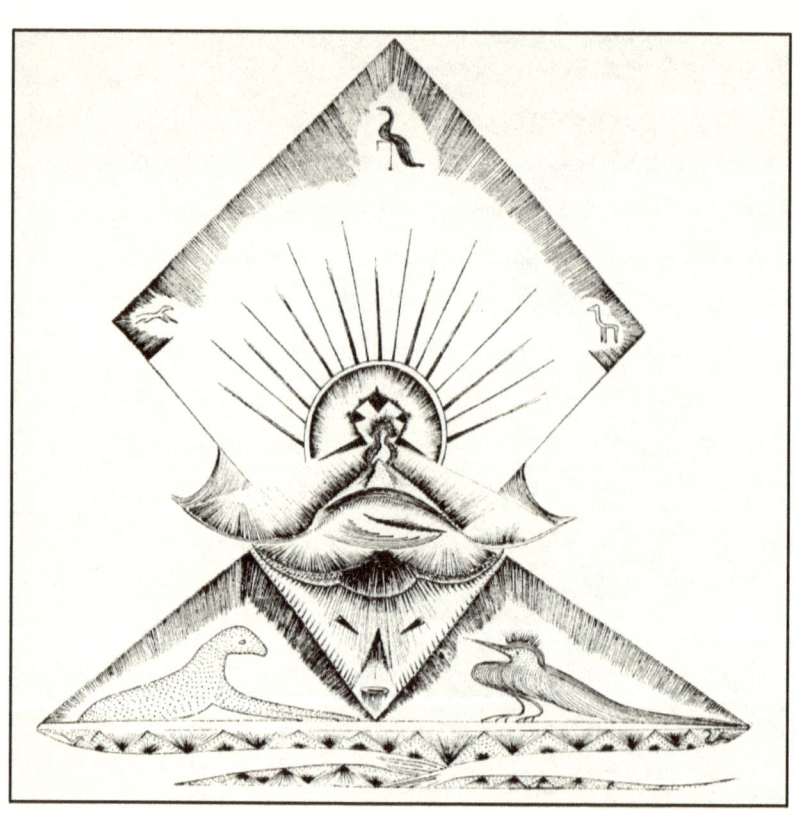

LUST FOR LIFE

◆ 1 ◆

To hell, to hell with balance! I break glasses; I want to *burn*, even if I break myself. I want to live only for ecstasy. Nothing else affects me. Small doses, moderate loves, all the *demi-teintes*—all these leave me cold. I like extravagance, heat…sexuality which bursts the thermometer! I'm neurotic, perverted, destructive, fiery, dangerous —lava, inflammable, unrestrained. I feel like a jungle animal who is escaping captivity.

—Incest, pg. 101

◆ 2 ◆

I look at my life as fiction, as an adventure story—something to be worked through.

—Conversations with Anaïs Nin, pp. 230-231

◆ 3 ◆

All the pleasure I take in luxury, I willingly surrender to that awesome, religious pleasure I get from creating life, hope, sanity, desire, hunger around me. I feel a deep pleasure when others enjoy. It is deeper than any other.

—Nearer the Moon, pg. 46

♦ 4 ♦

I am the kind of dangerous dreamer who executes all his reveries, wishes, words, promises, plans. The wildest and the lightest. A wish for me is not a game: it's a creation.

—Diary 2, pg. 192

♦ 5 ♦

It took me a lifetime to know that happiness is a quiet thing, not a peak of ecstasy.

—Diary of Others, 1955

♦ 6 ♦

When I first faced pain I was shattered. When I first met failure, defeat, denial, loss, death, I died. Not today. I believe in my power, in my magic, and I do not die. I survive, I love, live, continue.

—Mirages, pg. 245

♦ 7 ♦

I get furious at stairways, furious at doors, at walls, furious at everyday life which interferes with the continuity of ecstasy.

—*House of Incest*, pg. 44

♦ 8 ♦

His life rushes onward in such torrential rhythm that...only angels and devils can catch the tempo of it.

—*Henry & June*, pg. 220

♦ 9 ♦

How can I accept a limited definable self when I feel, in me, all possibilities?... I never feel the four walls around the substance of the self, the core. I feel only space. Illimitable space.

—*Diary 1*, pg. 200

♦ 10 ♦

Drunkenness... I would like to give you this gift...

—*Reunited*, pg. 138

♦ 11 ♦

I do not perceive people in their ordinary lives, but in their potentialities, their possibilities. And this vision often calls for and produces the gifts I expect.

—Reunited, pg. 93

♦ 12 ♦

Life is rich. It is a high adventure. Though I double the dose of my sedatives, it is no use. I'm dancing inside myself with a new bliss.

—Early Diary 4, pg. 489

♦ 13 ♦

No desire of the body, but for what lies in there, what lies in the flesh, the world, the thought, the creation, the illumination.

—Fire, pg. 207

♦ 14 ♦

Hell is a different place for each man, or each man has his own particular hell. My descent into the inferno is a descent into the irrational level of existence, where the instincts and blind emotions are loose, where one lives by pure impulse, pure fantasy, and therefore pure madness.

—Diary 1, pg. 36

◆ 15 ◆

I have created myself a soul, big as the world, that leaks all over,
and I have to keep calling for the plumber.

—Fire, pg. 128

◆ 16 ◆

I hope I have the courage to die alone, not to drag others into the
caves to hold my hand. Particularly if you decide to die
continuously, or to be dead in life—you should not expect
company. If you are going to bury yourself alive—and plenty of
people do—you should not demand the companionship of the
living.

—Diary of Others, 1956

◆ 17 ◆

I, with a deeper instinct, choose friends who arouse my energy,
who make enormous demands on me, who are capable of
enriching me with experience, pain, people who do not doubt my
courage, or my toughness…but who challenge my keenest wisdom,
who have the courage to treat me like a woman in spite of the fact
they are aware of my vulnerability.

—Diary 1, pg. 132

◆ 18 ◆

I walk ahead of myself in perpetual expectancy of miracles.

—House of Incest, pg. 40

◆ 19 ◆

Do you know what I would answer to someone who asked me for a description of myself, in a hurry? This:

?? !!

For indeed my life is a perpetual question mark—my thirst for books, my observations of people, all tend to satisfy a great, overwhelming desire to know, to understand, to find an answer to a million questions. And gradually the answers are revealed, many things are explained, and above all, many things are given *names* and *described*, and my restlessness is subdued. Then I become an *exclamatory* person, clapping my hands to the immense surprises the world holds for me, and falling from one ecstasy into another. I have the habit of peeping and prying and listening and seeking— passionate curiosity and expectation. But I have also the habit of *being surprised*, the habit of being filled with wonder and satisfaction *each time* I stumble on some wondrous thing.

—Early Diary 2, pg. 146

♦ 20 ♦

I walk into the fire always, and come out more alive.

—Diary 4, pg. 177

♦ 21 ♦

I want to trespass boundaries, erase all identifications, anything which fixes one permanently into one mold, one place, without hope of change.

—A Spy in the House of Love, from *Cities of the Interior,* pg. 458

♦ 22 ♦

I was not traveling away from human life, I was seeking my own fulfillment. Searching for heightened moments uninterrupted by life's daily exigencies.

—Diary 3, pg. 301

♦ 23 ♦

I'm awaiting a lover. I have to be rent and pulled apart and live according to the demons and the imagination in me. I'm restless. Things are calling me away. My hair is being pulled by the stars again.

—Fire, pg. 101

◆ 24 ◆

Life forces me to prevent and remedy needs—to be a cosmos all by myself: man, woman, father, mother, lover, mistress, child. All the roles!

—Fire, pg. 44

◆ 25 ◆

Of course you are hurt by jealousy or envy or even lack of full appreciation. Of course you are vulnerable to people and the absence of generosity. But to live in spite of this, to love life so much, one is willing to be wounded.

—Joyous Transformation, 1969

◆ 26 ◆

You give your life, your whole life, to bourgeois demands and in return you have a bed and good food, but no leisure, no time to live as you wish.

—Diary of Others, 1956

◆ 27 ◆

I never accept being pinned down by a catastrophe. I think of the future. I *displace* myself… My imagination takes me away from the eye of the cyclone.

—Diary 7, pg. 304

Lust for Life

◆ 28 ◆

Save me from beatification, from the horrors of static perfection.
Precipitate me into the inferno.

—Henry & June, pg. 104

◆ 29 ◆

I palliate the sufferings of others. Yes, I see myself always softening
the blows, dissolving acids, neutralizing poisons, every moment of
the day. I try to fulfill the wishes of others, to perform miracles. I
exert myself performing miracles.

—Diary 1, pg. 65

◆ 30 ◆

Please understand…that I am in full rebellion against my own
mind, that when I *live*, I live by impulse, by emotion, by white
heat…

—A Literate Passion, pg. 8

◆ 31 ◆

The impetus to grow and live intensely is so powerful in me I
cannot resist it. I will work, I will love my husband, but I will fulfill
myself.

—Henry & June, pg. 1

The real wonders of life lie in the depths. Exploring the depths for truths is the real wonder which the child and the artist know: magic and power lie in truth.

—Diary 4, pg. 121

The secret of a full life is to live and relate to others as if they might not be there tomorrow, as if you might not be there tomorrow. It eliminates the vice of procrastination, the sin of postponement, failed communications, failed communions. This thought has made me more and more attentive to all encounters, meetings, introductions, which might contain the seed of depth that might be carelessly overlooked. This feeling has become a rarity, and rarer every day now that we have reached a hastier and more superficial rhythm, now that we believe we are in touch with a greater amount of people, more people, more countries. This is the illusion which might cheat us of being in touch deeply with the one breathing next to us. The dangerous time when mechanical voices, radios, telephones, take the place of human intimacies, and the concept of being in touch with millions brings a greater and greater poverty in intimacy and human vision.

—Diary 4, pp. 148-149

◆ 34 ◆

The wine running down my throat—passing through the throat of the world. The warmth of the day like a man's hand on my breasts, the smell of the street like a man's breath on my neck.

—*The Winter of Artifice,* Paris edition, pg. 30

◆ 35 ◆

We cannot forget that every one of our lives is an adventure. In every one of our lives there is a possibility of escape, of expansion, of growth, of sublimation, of transcending the obstacles which seem absolutely impossible to move.

—*A Woman Speaks,* pg. 221

◆ 36 ◆

There is a fantastic courage in this, to live without laws, without fetters, without thought of consequences.

—*Diary 1,* pg. 45

◆ 37 ◆

Can one multiply, share, expand without loss of substance? I answered my own question. Yes, if you can extend feeling into all you do, say, write. If in one minute spent with a stranger you can create the annihilation of strangeness.

—Diary 7, pg. 244

◆ 38 ◆

Everyone who comes to the door I begin by *liking*, by being open to their invisible messages, by seeking links, correlations, affinities, by seeking to know them.

—Joyous Transformation, 1973

◆ 39 ◆

I always have difficulty with people who are not openly warm, expressive. I need a certain sign, a certain invitation.

—Diary 3, pg. 158

This hunger which had inhabited her entire being, which had thinned her blood, transpired through her bones, attacked the roots of her hair, given a fragility to her skin which was never to disappear entirely, had been so enormous that it had marked her whole being and her eyes with an indelible mark. Although her life changed and every want was filled later, this appearance of hunger remained. As if nothing could ever quite fill it. Her being had received no sun, no food, no air, no warmth, no love. It retained open pores of yearning and longing, mysterious spongy cells of absorption. The space between actuality, absolute deprivation, and the sumptuosity of her imagination could never be entirely covered. What she had created in the void, in the emptiness, in the bareness continued to shame all that was offered her, and her large, infinitely blue eyes continued to assert the immensity of her hunger.

—*Ladders to Fire*, in *Cities of the Interior*, pg. 28

◆ 41 ◆

Touched bottom again. Decided to liberate myself... We are never trapped unless we choose to be.

—*Diary 4*, pg. 32

◆ 42 ◆

Warmth, perfume, rugs, soft lights, books. They do not appease me. I am aware of time passing, of all the world contains that I have not seen, of all the interesting people I have not met.

—Diary 3, pg. 254

◆ 43 ◆

We all have dual wishes, dual selves. A flashy side which wants to be noticed and famous, and a quiet side which only wants to be left alone in peace to work. My resolution was always: Do them all, they are all you; embrace them all.

—Diary 7, pg. 241

◆ 44 ◆

It's a million times better to risk being deserted or betrayed than to withdraw into a fortress of alienation, shut the door and break the contact with others. Because then we really die. That is death. That is emotional death.

—A Woman Speaks, pg. 10

◆ 45 ◆

When human pain has struck me fiercely, when anger has corroded me, I rise, I always rise after the crucifixion, and I am in terror of my ascensions.

—House of Incest, pg. 37

◆ 46 ◆

Over and over again I sail towards joy, which is never in the room with me, but always near me, across the way, like those rooms full of gayety one sees from the street, or the gayety in the street one sees from a window. Will I ever reach joy? It hides behind the turning merry-go-round of the traveling circus. As soon as I approach it, it is no longer joy. Joy is a foam, an illumination. I am poorer and hungrier for the want of it. When I am in the dance, joy is outside in the elusive garden. When I am in the garden, I hear it exploding from the house. When I am traveling, joy settles like an aurora borealis over the land I leave. When I stand on the shore I see it bloom on the flag of a departing ship. What joy? Have I not possessed it? I want the joy of simple colors, street organs, ribbons, flags, not a joy that takes my breath away and throws me into space alone where no one else can breathe with me, not the joy that comes from a lonely drunkenness. There are so many joys, but I have only known the ones that come like a miracle, touching everything with light.

—Mirages, pg. 3

◆ 47 ◆

I began the day in a golden mood which I carried like a fragile egg. I carried it against my breast, warming it. I carried it to Hans to awaken him, to present him with it, to tell him it was a tropical day, to bring him out into the sun. I offered him my mood like another gift.

—*The Winter of Artifice,* Paris edition, pg. 60

◆ 48 ◆

What I corrupted was what is called the truth in favor of a more marvelous world.

—*A Spy in the House of Love*, from *Cities of the Interior*, pg. 457

◆ 49 ◆

When he first stepped out of the car and walked towards the door where I stood waiting, I saw a man I liked. In his writing he is flamboyant, virile, animal, magnificent. He's a man whom life makes drunk, I thought. He is like me.

—*Henry & June*, pg. 6

◆ 50 ◆

I have decided that if analysis is a hothouse, a hastening of wisdom and growth, nevertheless the life experience must be actually lived out and through, completely, in spite of it; everything that is lived out in the imagination is poison.

—*Fire*, pg. 49

◆ 51 ◆

The youthful spirit wins over the face and body.

—*Diary 7*, pg. 299

◆ 52 ◆

I am not always just living, just following all my fantasies; I come up for air, for understanding.

—*Henry & June*, pg. 44

◆ 53 ◆

Self-assertion. Unjust—cruel—necessary. I must be true to myself—there is a *savage* in me—there is a primitive woman— there is a *savage*. No pity.

—*Reunited*, pg. 128

The physical as a symbol of the spiritual world. The people who keep old rags, old useless objects, who hoard, accumulate: are they also keepers and hoarders of old ideas, useless information, lovers of the past only, even in its form of detritus? ...I have the opposite obsession. In order to change skins, evolve into new cycles, I feel one has to learn to discard. If one changes internally, one should not continue to live with the same objects. They reflect one's mind and psyche of yesterday. I throw away what has no dynamic, living use. I keep nothing to remind me of the passage of time, deterioration, loss, shriveling.

—*Diary 4*, pg. 26

My dream now doesn't concern just me anymore; it has to do with all women. My dream at the moment is to see women really grow and expand to their full, absolutely fullest capacity.

—*A Woman Speaks*, pg. 260

LOVE AND SENSUALITY

◆ 56 ◆

If I have genius, it is a genius for loving. This journal could be a manual of love, passionate love, fleshly love, understanding love, pitying, maternal, intellectual, artistic, creative, non-human...

—Reunited, pg. 66

◆ 57 ◆

Even if you don't mean it, just for tonight, say you love me. I won't ever remind you of it; I will not see you again, but just for tonight say you love me, say you love me.

—Seduction of the Minotaur, from *Cities of the Interior*, pg. 514

◆ 58 ◆

We looked at each other across miles and miles of separation. Our eyes did not meet. His thoughts enwrapped him in glass.

—The Winter of Artifice, Paris edition, pp. 155-156

♦ 59 ♦

When you're in my arms, I know you're mine. But your feet are so swift, so swift, they carry you as lightly as wings, I never know where, too fast, too fast away from me.

—The Four-Chambered Heart, in *Cities of the Interior*, pg. 250

♦ 60 ♦

His hunger was contagious; it gave birth to hunger, and with the hunger the savour of all things was restored. His appetite made things alive. It seemed to stir the activity of the earth, to call out vigorous sprouting of the earth's driest crust. It was like water over a desert, the moisture of his sensual mouth, the moisture of his sensual desires.

—The Winter of Artifice, Paris edition, pg. 48

♦ 61 ♦

When the train moved, his legs and arms seemed to melt together into one tense, single, upright line, like the spire of a cathedral—a coalescence, a unification. And all his mood, feeling and thought and blood converged to one point…to a synthesis of feeling in his eyes. As I moved away it was as if I were drinking his life. He offered it all, all in one bouquet, all tied, drawn, melted into one yearning.

—Reunited, pg. 26

Love and Sensuality

◆ 62 ◆

By desiring someone who would not desire her, she could allow
this fire to burn and feel: how alive I am! I am capable of desire.

—*Seduction of the Minotaur*, in *Cities of the Interior*, pg. 563

◆ 63 ◆

Real sensuality has no need of stimulants.

—*Diary 1*, pg. 252

◆ 64 ◆

And in his eyes he had the look of the cat who inspires a desire to
caress but loves no one, who never feels he must respond to the
impulses he arouses.

—*Delta of Venus*, pg. 18

◆ 65 ◆

We hold on to each other as if to make the penetration permanent
against all the separations demanded by life.

—*Trapeze*, pg. 56

As soon as I kiss him I know that I love him with a blind instinct beyond all reason, with all his defects.

—*Fire*, pg. 12

Only the pagan can enjoy his sensual life like a fruit.

—*Diary of Others*, 1955

At night too she puzzled the mystery of her desperate need of kindness. As other girls prayed for handsomeness in a lover, or for wealth, or for power, or for poetry, she had prayed fervently: let him be kind.

—*The Four-Chambered Heart*, in *Cities of the Interior*, pg. 376

He has, like me, a sense of smell. I let him inhale me, then I slip away.

—*Henry & June*, pg. 9

I love when you say: all that happens is *good*, it is *good*. I say all
that happens is *wonderful*. For me it is all symphonic, and I am so
aroused by living…in you alone I have found the same swelling of
enthusiasm, the same quick rising of the blood, the fullness…
Before, I almost used to think there was something wrong.
Everybody else seemed to have the *brakes on*… I never feel the
brakes. I overflow. And when I feel your excitement about life
flaring, next to mine, then it makes me dizzy.

—*A Literate Passion*, pg. 36

I love your silences, they are like mine. You are the only being
before whom I am not distressed by my own silences. You have a
vehement silence, one feels it is charged with essences, it is a
strangely alive silence, like a trap open over a well, from which one
can hear the secret murmur of the earth itself.

—*Under a Glass Bell*, pp. 51-52

I don't hear your words: your voice reverberates against my body
like another kind of caress, another kind of penetration. I have no
power over your voice. It comes straight from you into me. I could
stuff my ears and it would find its way into my blood and make it
rise.

—*Henry & June*, pp. 66-67

◆ 73 ◆

I refuse to die again as I died over John, so I am more wary of absolutism. I always leave a loophole, a way of escape.

I hate to feel that my incapacity to face the greatest pains of love is making me afraid of absolutism.

—*Incest*, pg. 98

◆ 74 ◆

I do not know death or indifference. Time kills nothing in me. I will die before my lovers and my memories. Each time a little bit of my flesh stirs somewhere...I will feel it in my body even though I have tried by art to deliver myself of all possessions.

A possessed being. Succubus and incubus of old loves. No dis-illusion, hatred, contempt kills love in me. This is my crucifixion.

—*Nearer the Moon*, pg. 322

◆ 75 ◆

I dreamed you; I wished for your existence. You will always be a part of my life. If I love you, it must be because we shared, at some moment, the same imaginings, the same madness, the same stage.

—*Diary 1*, pg. 21

Love and Sensuality

♦ 76 ♦

I feel a little like the moon who took possession of you for a moment and then returned your soul to you. You should not love me. One ought not to love the moon. If you come too near me, I will hurt you.

—Delta of Venus, pg. 138

♦ 77 ♦

I had to make the journey back to him, not across three thousand miles of land, but a million light years of the subtle space between our thoughts.

—Diary of Others, 1957

♦ 78 ♦

I love her for what she has dared to be, for her hardness, her cruelty, her egoism, her perverseness, her demoniac destructive-ness. She would crush me to ashes without hesitation. She is a personality created to the limit. I worship her courage to hurt, and I am willing to be sacrificed to it. She will add the sum of me to her.

—Henry & June, pg. 19

◆ 79 ◆

I prefer empty cages, Sabina, until I find a unique bird I once saw in my dreams.

—*A Spy in the House of Love*, in *Cities of the Interior*, pg. 432

◆ 80 ◆

I want to fall in love in such a way that the mere sight of a man, even a block away from me, will shake and pierce me, will weaken me, and make me tremble and soften and melt. That is how I want to fall in love, so hard the mere thought of him will bring on an orgasm.

—*Delta of Venus*, pg. 72

◆ 81 ◆

Do not believe the red journal. You don't know yet when and how I fell in love with you. That's in the purple journal.

—*A Literate Passion*, pg. 61

◆ 82 ◆

Imperceptibly at times he withdrew, just slightly, as if to make room for the contractions, which pressed him and lured him back into the depths of her.

—*Auletris*, pg. 17

Love and Sensuality

With my journal, I was able to break through and say to you: here is the *human* me. The next day there were veils again, but you broke through them. And then the kiss, and then…and then.

—*A Literate Passion*, pg. 77

The drug of love was no escape, for in its coils lie latent dreams of greatness which awaken when men and women fecundate each other deeply. Something is always born of man and woman lying together and exchanging the essences of their lives. Some seed is always carried and opened in the soil of passion. The fumes of desire are the womb of man's birth and often in the drunkenness of caresses history is made, and science, and philosophy. For a woman, as she sews, cooks, embraces, covers, warms, also dreams that the man taking her will be more than a man, will be the mythological figure of her dreams, the hero, the discoverer, the builder... Unless she is the anonymous whore, no man enters woman with impunity, for where the seed of man and woman mingle, within the drops of blood exchanged, the changes that take place are the same as those of great flowing rivers of inheritance, which carry traits of character from father to son to grandson, traits of character as well as physical traits.

—*The Four-Chambered Heart*, in *Cities of the Interior*, pg. 277

♦ 85 ♦

It was as if her fingers had called forth a hidden source of moisture, touched off the secret holder of woman's perfume.

—*Auletris*, pg. 27

♦ 86 ♦

Jeunes filles are for the daytime, but autumnal women are for the night.

—*Diary of Others*, 1957

♦ 87 ♦

Love demands polarity, not similarity.

—*Reunited*, pg. 19

♦ 88 ♦

Men can be in love with literary figures, with poetic and mythological figures, but let them meet with Artemis, with Venus, with any of the goddesses of love, and then they start hurling moral judgments.

—*Diary 1*, pp. 245-246

No moment of charm without long roots in the past, no moment of charm is born on bare soil, a careless accident of beauty, but is the sum of great sorrows, growths, and efforts.

But love, the great narcotic, was the hothouse in which all the selves burst into their fullest bloom…

love the great narcotic was the revealer in the alchemist's bottle rendering visible the most untraceable substances

love the great narcotic was the *agent provocateur* exposing all the secret selves to daylight

love the great narcotic-lined fingertips with clairvoyance

pumped iridescence into the lungs for transcendental x-rays

printed new geographies in the lining of eyes

adorned words with sails, ears with velvet mutes

and soon the balcony tipped their shadows into the river, too, so that the kiss might be baptized in the holy waters of continuity.

—*The Four-Chambered Heart*, in *Cities of the Interior*, pg. 245

My trapeze is working, I have not fallen off, the two lives are kept separate, and I retain my sanity.

—*Trapeze*, pg. 103

◆ 91 ◆

Only love begets love.

—*Diary 7*, pg. 90

◆ 92 ◆

You are the poet, you walk inside my dreams, I love the pain and the flame in you, but do not touch me.

—*Under a Glass Bell*, pg. 54

◆ 93 ◆

She twisted herself like a python, jerked herself in all directions as if she were being burnt or beaten. Powerful muscles gave to her motions a strength which stirred the most bestial desires.

—*Delta of Venus*, pg. 155

◆ 94 ◆

Our love of each other was like two long shadows kissing without hope of reality.

—*House of Incest*, pg. 48

Pure love, pure friendship—these are ideals. These may exist now and then, and they are beautiful things to behold. But they are not goals. They are phenomenal and accidental.

—*A Literate Passion*, pg. 184

Sensual love can continue as long as emotional love is alive.

—*Joyous Transformation*, 1973

Sex loses all its power and magic when it becomes explicit, mechanical, overdone, when it becomes a mechanistic obsession. It becomes a bore. You have taught us more than anyone I know how wrong it is not to mix it with emotion, hunger, desire, lust, whims, caprices, personal ties, deeper relationships which change its color, flavor, rhythms, intensities.

—*Diary 3*, pg. 177

I had forced the hour glass of pain to turn. We had run after each other. We had tried to possess each other. We had been slaves of a pattern, and not of love.

—*The Winter of Artifice*, Paris edition, pg. 195

For you and for me the highest moment, the keenest joy, is not
when our minds dominate but when we lose our minds.

—*Henry & June*, pg. 47

She was truthful, or I was the greatest dupe who ever existed. I can
only believe in our ecstasy. I don't want to know, I only want to
love her.

—*Henry & June*, pg. 269

The true liberation of eroticism lies in accepting the fact that there
are a million facets to it, a million forms of eroticism, a million
objects of it, situations, atmosphere, and variations.

—*In Favor of the Sensitive Man*, pg. 11

The potion drunk by lovers is prepared by no one but themselves.
The potion is the sum of one's whole existence.

—*The Four-Chambered Heart*, in *Cities of the Interior*, pg. 244

◆ 103 ◆

He took charge of the dinner. I sat far from him on the couch. We did not talk very long. His eyes were wet and glistening, and he was hungry for caresses. The radio was playing the love scene of *Tristan and Isolde*. We stood up. My mood was, above all, amazement—to see this beautiful, incredible face over mine, and to find in this slender, dreamy, remote young man a burst of electric passion.

— Trapeze, pg. 2

◆ 104 ◆

The voices that carried us into serenity, the voices which made the drum beat in us, sex, sex, sex, sex, desire, the bow of the violins passing between the legs, the curves of women's backs yielding, the baton of the orchestra leader, the second voice of locked instruments, the strings snapping, the dissonances, the hardness, the flute weeping.

— The Winter of Artifice, Paris edition, pg. 145

◆ 105 ◆

Then at certain moments I remember one of his words and I suddenly feel the sensual woman flaring up, as if violently caressed. I say the word to myself, with joy. It is at such a moment that my true body lives.

—Henry & June, pg. 50

◆ 106 ◆

I think the only taboos should be on not loving.

—*A Woman Speaks*, pg. 61

◆ 107 ◆

You love so to be against things. I love to be *for* things. You make caricatures. It takes great hate to make caricatures. I elect, I love— the welling of love stifles me at night—as in that dream which you struggled to make *real* yesterday—to nail down, yes, with your engulfing kiss.

—*A Literate Passion*, pg. 21

◆ 108 ◆

The leaf fall of her words, the stained glass hues of her moods, the rust in her voice, the smoke in her mouth, her breath on my vision like human breath blinding a mirror.

—*House of Incest*, pg. 24

◆ 109 ◆

For people who are twins, there is always a curse on their love.

—*Reunited*, pg. 223

Love and Sensuality

There are a million ways of making love, but there is only one
which happens miraculously, one of such intense merging that
body and soul seem to fuse.

—Joyous Transformation, 1976

They lay entangled, his naked body the whole length of her, and
she flung back, legs apart, and eyes closed, and their mouths
together.

—Auletris, pg. 17

Sex does not thrive on monotony. Without feeling, inventions,
moods, no surprises in bed. Sex must be mixed with tears, laughter,
words, promises, scenes, jealousy, envy, all the spices of fear,
foreign travel, new faces, novels, stories, dreams, fantasies, music,
dancing, opium, wine.

—Diary 3, pp. 177-178

Eroticism is one of the basic means of self-knowledge, as basic
as poetry.

—In Favor of the Sensitive Man, pg. 22

Things I forgot to tell you: The *quena* is an instrument like a flute used by the South American Indians. It is made of human bones. It owes its origin to the worship of an Indian for his mistress. When she died he made a flute of one of her bones. It has a more penetrating, more haunting sound than the ordinary flute.

That I love you, and that when I awake in the morning I use my intelligence to discover more ways of appreciating you.

That when June comes back she will love you more because I have loved you. There are new leaves on the tip and climax of your already overrich head.

That I love you.

That I love you.

That I love you.

I have become an idiot like Gertrude Stein. That's what love does to intelligent women. They cannot write letters anymore.

—*A Literate Passion*, pg. 64

Very slowly, with hands, tongues, mouths, we unwrapped and untied ourselves, laying open gifts. Gave birth to each other again, as separate bodies who enjoy collision.

—*Fire*, pg. 2

Love and Sensuality

◆ 116 ◆

Was it not an act of love to impersonate the loved one?

—Seduction of the Minotaur, in *Cities of the Interior,* pg. 555

◆ 117 ◆

Hans and I were devouring each other in a dark banquet of teeth into flesh, and flesh soldered together by currents of ever-returning desires.

—Auletris, pg. 81

◆ 118 ◆

We did not touch each other. We were both leaning over the abyss.

—Henry & June, pg. 55

◆ 119 ◆

We efface an hour by passionate love, without twists, without aftertaste. When it is finished, it is not finished, we lie still in each other's arms lulled by our love, by tenderness—sensuality in which the whole being can participate.

—Henry & June, pg. 10

◆ 120 ◆

We may seem to forget a person, a place, a state of being, a past life, but meanwhile what we are doing is selecting new actors, seeking the closest reproduction to the friend, the lover, the husband we are trying to forget, in order to re-enact the drama with understudies. And one day we open our eyes and there we are, repeating the same story. How could it be otherwise? The design comes from within us. It is internal. It is what the old mystics described as karma, repeated until the spiritual or emotional experience was understood, liquidated, achieved.

—*Seduction of the Minotaur,* in *Cities of the Interior,* pg. 558

◆ 121 ◆

We give to our friends only a small part of ourselves. In the climate of love another being emerges.

—*Diary 3,* pg. 139

◆ 122 ◆

We stood before the night which belonged to us as two women emerging out of sleep. We stood on the first step of our timidity, of our faith, before the long night which belonged to us. Blameless of original sin, of literary sins, of the sin of calculation, of premeditation, or of experience.

—*The Winter of Artifice,* Paris edition, pg. 102

What you burnt, broke, and tore is still in my hands. I am the keeper of fragile things and I have kept of you what is indissoluble.

—*House of Incest*, pg. 27

When does real love begin?

At first it was a fire, eclipses, short circuits, lightning and fireworks; then incense, hammocks, drugs, wines, perfumes; then spasm and honey, fever, fatigue, warmth, currents of liquid fire, feast and orgies; then dreams, visions, candlelight, flowers, pictures; then images out of the past, fairy tales, stories, then pages out of a book, a poem; then laughter, then chastity.

At what moment does the knife wound sink so deep that the flesh begins to weep with love?

At first power, power, then the wound, and love, and love and fears, and the loss of the self, and the gift, and slavery. At first I ruled, loved less; then more, then slavery. Slavery to his image, his odor, the craving, the hunger, the thirst, the obsession.

—*Fire*, pp. 289-290

I've found the one I can play with, play really, play the woman, play everything in my head or body with a blood rhythm.

—*Fire*, pg. 2

♦ 126 ♦

When he lay over me with his unabatable attentiveness I knew he
was watching the alterations of my face, listening to the cries I
uttered, and the final deeper, savage tones. I closed my eyes before
this watchfulness of his and sank into a blind, moist drunkenness. I
felt myself caught in the immense jaws of his desire, felt myself
dissolving, ripping open to his descent. I felt myself yielding up to
his dark hunger. An immense jaw closing upon my feelings, my
feelings smouldering, rising from me like smoke from a black mass.
Take me, take me, take my gifts and my moods and my body, take
all you want.

— *The Winter of Artifice*, Paris edition, pp. 47-48

♦ 127 ♦

I will be the one woman you will never have…excessive living
weighs down the imagination: we will not live, we will only write
and talk to swell the sails.

—*A Literate Passion*, pg. 16

♦ 128 ♦

One cannot be both sensitive and invulnerable.

—*Diary 7*, pg. 89

◆ 129 ◆

When she closed her eyes she felt he had many hands, which touched her everywhere, and many mouths, which passed so swiftly over her, and with a wolflike sharpness, his teeth sank into her fleshiest parts. Naked now, he lay his full length over her. She enjoyed his weight on her, enjoyed being crushed under his body. She wanted him soldered to her, from mouth to feet. Shivers passed through her body.

—Delta of Venus, pg. 98

◆ 130 ◆

When we walked together through the streets, bodies close together, arm in arm, hands locked, I could not talk. We were walking over the world, over reality, into ecstasy. When she smelled my handkerchief, she inhaled me. When I clothed her beauty, I possessed her.

—Henry & June, pg. 25

◆ 131 ◆

I can no longer love what hurts me.

—Diary of Others, 1957

◆ 132 ◆

Your beauty drowns me, drowns the core of me. When your beauty burns me I dissolve as I never dissolved before man. From all men I was different, and myself, but I see in you that part of me which is you. I feel you in me, I feel my own voice becoming heavier, as if I were drinking you in, every delicate thread of resemblance being soldered by fire and one no longer detects the fissure.

—House of Incest, pp. 25-26

◆ 133 ◆

I was awake last night telling you—all night—of that man I discovered yesterday...the man I sense with my feelings the first moment—all the mountains of words, writing, quotations have sundered—I only know now the splendor, the blinding splendor of your room—and that unreal moment—how can a moment be at once so unreal and so warm—so warm.

—A Literate Passion, pg. 21

◆ 134 ◆

Why does a gesture, a walk, stir your blood? What a mystery this is, desire. The love sickness, the sensitivity, the obsession, the flutter of the heart, the ebb and flow of the blood. There is no drug and no alcohol to equal it.

—Diary 3, pg. 274

Love and Sensuality

◆ 135 ◆

Henry, we are going to taste *all* we can give each other before June comes, quickly, deeply—we are going to lie together as often as possible. It is all fragile, but for every day of it I am thankful, thankful!

—*A Literate Passion*, pg. 48

◆ 136 ◆

As she came towards me from the darkness of my garden into the light of the doorway I saw for the first time the most beautiful woman on earth.

—*Henry & June*, pg. 14

◆ 137 ◆

With her eyes alone she could give this response, this absolutely erotic response, as if febrile waves were trembling there, pools of madness...something devouring that could lick a man all over like a flame, annihilate him, with a pleasure never known before.

—*Little Birds*, pg. 96

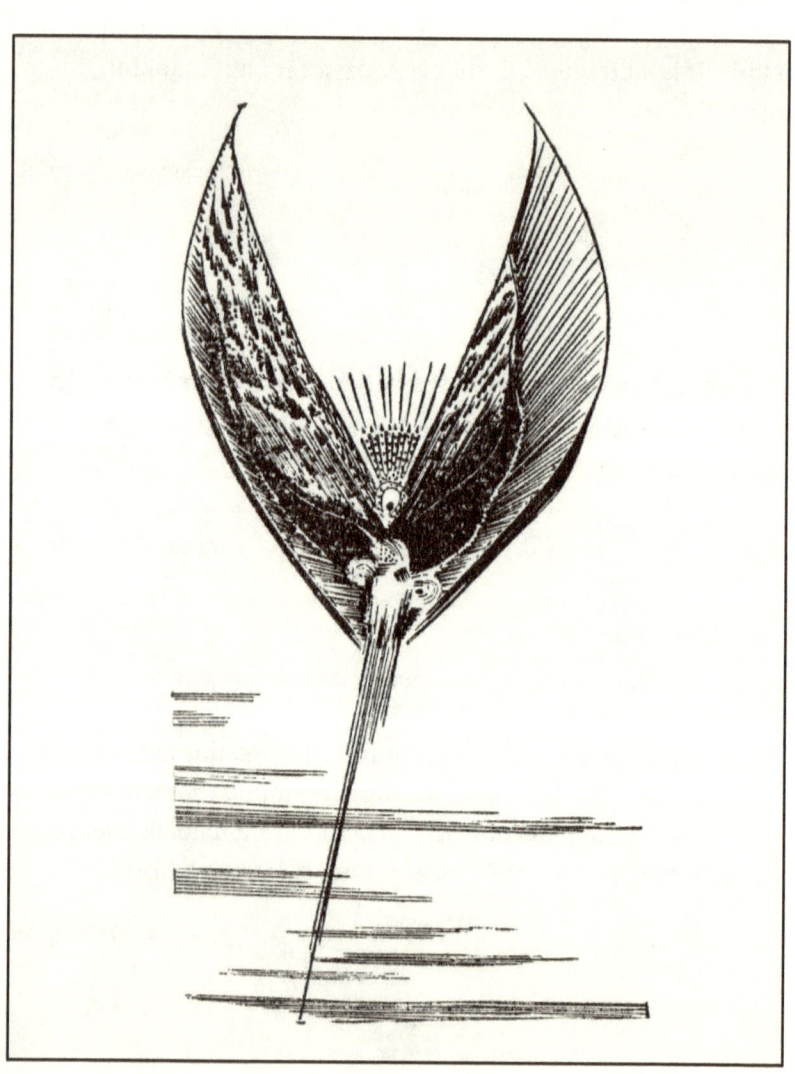

CONSCIOUSNESS

◆ 138 ◆

When you hold on to your own true character, people cannot interfere with your growth.

—Trapeze, pg. 197

◆ 139 ◆

America and Russia will one day fall into each other's arms. They have both destroyed the same values.

—Diary of Others, 1955

◆ 140 ◆

There was once a woman who had one hundred faces. She showed one face to each person, and so it took one hundred men to write her biography.

—Early Diary 4, pg. 419

◆ 141 ◆

I have to create an inner world because I reject this one. It is not mine.

—Diary of Others, 1955

◆ 142 ◆

I hear the train whistle at night and the coyotes in a pack with their thin wailing cries answer the train, mistaking it for another animal in the night… In America the vast spaces accentuate the vast spaces between people, deserts which stretch between human beings. It is a void which has to be spanned by the automobile. It takes an hour to reach a movie, two hours to reach a friend. So the coyotes howl and wail at the awful emptiness of mountains, deserts, hills.

—Diary 5, pg. 72

◆ 143 ◆

The freedom of America is an illusion. Transplanted from Europe, I was fully aware of the opposite of freedom in the air, so much Puritan disapproval, so much of the spectator and voyeur, watching one live and jealous of those who live. So much negative criticism, so much hidden hostility, like the hostilities of old maids locked in small towns who sent poison letters and persecuted lovers.

A sin to look inward, they feel, and yet that is why there is so much loss of identity. A sin to be personal, and yet that is why there is so much loneliness and alienation.

—Diary 7, pg. 46

◆ 144 ◆

If you don't grow, you die inside. A dead woman can make no one happy.

—Diary of Others, 1962

Consciousness

◆ 145 ◆

The persona is something we create defensively. It's what we present to the world, what we think the world will accept. We all do this to a certain extent, but I don't think that we can ever really communicate on the basis of persona to persona. Thus, we become lonely within the persona.

—Conversations with Anaïs Nin, pp. 244-245

◆ 146 ◆

Neurosis is "possession." You are possessed by devils of destruction. They drive you. They make you compulsive. They make you destroy. It is not your voice, your true self. But it inhabits your body. It is the spirit of the past. It is the past selves superimposing themselves over the present, blurring it, choking it.

—Diary 5, pg. 234

◆ 147 ◆

If Europe exploited the people and kept them poor, America has committed a greater crime: it enriches them but exploits their ignorance, denies them education and refinement and erases growth. It exploits them as buyers to their salesmanship.

—Diary of Others, 1956

◆ 148 ◆

I think we can make our own imaginative world and fantasy world, our own philosophy and our own religion from whatever is in *us*.

—*Conversations with Anaïs Nin*, pg. 64

◆ 149 ◆

The romantic and the neurotic are the same thing; neither allows you to make real relationships. In other words, we impose these roles on others and then we demand certain things.

—*Conversations with Anaïs Nin*, pg. 69

◆ 150 ◆

It is in the moments of emotional crisis that human beings reveal themselves most accurately.

—*The Novel of the Future*, pg. 159

◆ 151 ◆

The end of one civilization *is* the beginning of another; they dovetail each other, just like the falling of withered flowers produce the seeds for the Spring.

—*A Literate Passion*, pg. 90

Consciousness

I don't believe in war, in any kind of war. War isn't going to solve the problems of our relationships, or affect our psychological independence, or our freedom to act, or our standard of living.

—Conversations with Anaïs Nin, pg. 247

Analysis is like a shock treatment, it throws you back into childhood in order to recapture the reparable elements, to reconstruct the personality. To reconstruct the personality it is necessary to find the original wound. You have to reevaluate the past so it will not remain an incubus or succubus.

—Diary 5, pg. 111

Politicians are as narrow-minded as priests. You can have no other love—so the rest of the personality is atrophied. At least in the drama of personal illusions, one recognizes the disillusionment with a lover, but meanwhile one has possessed life and pleasure. In politics one has possessed nothing.

—Diary of Others, 1955

◆ 155 ◆

Whatever you approach with hostility you'll never get to know, you can never come close to it.

—A Woman Speaks, pg. 249

◆ 156 ◆

Americans fear death because they try to live without the past. The past is comforting as it is not ashes at all, but an eternal flame whose light illumines our spirit and defers death, incites us to live.

—Joyous Transformation, 1974

◆ 157 ◆

We will always have a conflict between our growth and our fear that the growth will overshadow or injure someone else. And what we have to do is to create our own private morality and our private ethics and our private faith, for that naturally means that if you're a sensitive person you're not going to destroy people around you.

—A Woman Speaks, pg. 256

◆ 158 ◆

Archaeologists of the soul never returned empty-handed.

—Seduction of the Minotaur, in *Cities of the Interior*, pg. 565

Dreams are a language we have to learn. It's still an indirect language because we can't bear the naked truth, so it comes in the form of a symbol or a metaphor.

—*A Woman Speaks*, pg. 130

What violence could never achieve, understanding does.

—*Joyous Transformation*, 1970

All of us carry seeds of anxieties left from childhood, but the determination to live with others in close and loving harmony can overcome all the obstacles, provided we have learned to *integrate the differences.*

—*In Favor of the Sensitive Man*, pg. 53

The media fabricate personalities and offer as false a vision of the world as we can possibly have. Although it sometimes serves us, most of the time it deceives us.

—*A Woman Speaks*, pg. 9

◆ 163 ◆

You cannot be revolutionary unless you know what you are rebelling for, not against, but for.

—Conversations with Anaïs Nin, pg. 39

◆ 164 ◆

As soon as one becomes strong one has to accept the consequences. Brave, strong ones are never pitied. People fight them… Today I am stronger and therefore I will be less gently treated.

—Incest, pg. 264

◆ 165 ◆

Every human being should push his development and skills and creativity as far as possible, as only then does one become valuable to the community, valuable to others. It is wrong to hold people back to remain on a level with the herd. We need explorers, adventurers, pathfinders, models, inventors.

—Diary 7, pg. 237

◆ 166 ◆

Analysis is not a duel of wits; it is an emotional drama, a primitive ritual in which the secret self is evoked.

—Diary of Others, 1957

Big business is the monster that will destroy everything, corrupt everything. It is a dehumanizing, corroding contemporary expression of all tyrannies, the Caesars, emperors, thugs and dictators.

—*Diary of Others*, 1957

Freedom means that no one is able to destroy you, enslave you, paralyze you.

—*Diary 7*, pg. 232

What a burden of guilt when a mother serves you, does all the menial tasks, feeds you, works for you, but then does not approve of what we become.

—*Diary 7*, pg. 232

When people quibble about little things, it is because they do not accept the big ones.

—*Diary of Others*, 1964

♦ 171 ♦

How often we make this circular journey into the past, linking fragments of an incomplete puzzle, seeing a complete image. What emerges is the change in our vision, the changes in our character, the errors, the blind spots. As we make the return journey it is not only to pass judgment on our past selves, it is to crystallize, reinforce, consolidate what we have gained.

—Diary 7, pg. 40

♦ 172 ♦

I am losing my great, dissolving, disintegrating pity for others, in which I saw deflected the compassion I wanted for myself. I no longer give compassion, which means I no longer need to receive it.

—Diary 1, pg. 300

♦ 173 ♦

I don't live here anymore. I live in the future.

—Diary 5, pg. 217

♦ 174 ♦

I have so much courage, fire, energy, for many things, yet I get so hurt, so wounded by small things.

—Nearer the Moon, pp. 92-93

◆ 175 ◆

I don't want you to taint that fragile coat of astonishing colors created by my illusions, which no painter has ever been able to reproduce. Strange, isn't it, that no chemical will give a human being the iridescence that illusions give them?

—*A Spy in the House of Love*, in *Cities of the Interior*, pg. 456

◆ 176 ◆

I long ago suspected violence grew out of powerlessness and humiliation. And America is the greatest humiliater in existence. It is always cultivating the power you get from humiliating others. It is the lowest form of power.

—*Joyous Transformation*, 1973

◆ 177 ◆

I have always been tormented by the image of multiplicity of selves. Some days I call it richness, and other days I see it as a disease, a proliferation as dangerous as cancer. My first concept about people around me was that all of them were coordinated into a WHOLE, whereas I was made up of a multitude of selves, of fragments.

—*Diary 1*, pg. 47

I have the power to multiply myself. I am not one woman.

—Early Diary 4, pg. 193

I am enmeshed in my lies, and I want absolution. I cannot tell the truth because I have felt the heads of men in my womb. The truth would be death-dealing and I prefer fairytales. I am wrapped in lies which do not penetrate my soul. As if the lies I tell were like costumes.

—House of Incest, pg. 40

I know that I go through life like a drunkard. I'm drunk on illusion. But no matter how drunk I am, there are things I can't help seeing, ferociously real things. I close my eyes, and I reel, I reel. I reel, I believe, I live in a fever and turmoil, I rise into ecstasy, but all the time there is the face of reality staring at me with ugly eyes. I know that if I open my eyes I will be intolerably hurt by the ugliness.

—Fire, pg. 50

◆ 181 ◆

Dwelling on age *is* aging.

—*Joyous Transformation*, 1974

◆ 182 ◆

I have such a fear of finding another like myself, and such a desire
to find one! I am so utterly lonely, but I also have such a fear that
my isolation be broken through, and I no longer be the head and
ruler of my universe.

—*House of Incest*, pp. 46-47

◆ 183 ◆

La condition humaine is what I have never accepted. That is why I
tried to create my own world.

—*Diary 5*, pg. 70

◆ 184 ◆

I identify with the deserted.

—*Diary of Others*, 1955

◆ 185 ◆

If a person continues to see only giants, it means he is still looking at the world through the eyes of a child.

—Diary 1, pg. 53

◆ 186 ◆

I want to clarify my life. I need truth. I know how to clarify the simple love of those who can look at each other in the face, who do not need to hide anything. The illusion doesn't have to feed on lies. The illusion is in the truth itself.

—Reunited, pg. 38

◆ 187 ◆

I prefer by far the warmth and softness to mere brilliancy and coldness. Some people remind me of sharp dazzling diamonds. Valuable but lifeless and loveless. Others, of the simplest field flowers, with hearts full of dew and with all the tints of celestial beauty reflected in their modest petals.

—Early Diary 2, pg. 7

◆ 188 ◆

I belong only to myself and to my work.

—Early Diary 4, pg. 462

Consciousness

Introspection does not need to be a still life. It can be an active alchemy.

—Diary 1, pg. 126

It is difficult to make friends with someone seeking other selves.

—Letters to a Friend in Australia, pg. 21

The struggle to make something great out myself without being egotistical is almost impossible to endure.

—Early Diary 4, pg. 251

The organization of the world is a task for realists. The poet and the workman will always be victims of power and interest. No world will ever be run by a mystic idea, because by the time it begins to *function* it ceases to be mystical. When the Catholic Church became a force, an organization, it ceased to be mystic! The realist always conquers the poetic as the human. Interest wins out. The world will always be ruled by soulless people and power.

—Fire, pp. 341-342

◆ 193 ◆

I know why families were created with all their imperfections. They humanize you. They are made to make you forget yourself occasionally, so that the beautiful balance of life is not destroyed.

—*Early Diary 3*, pg. 220

◆ 194 ◆

I have a mind which is bigger than all the rest of me, an inexorable conscience.

—*Henry & June*, pg. 34

◆ 195 ◆

I had been struck by the analogy between neurosis and romanticism. Romanticism was truly a parallel to neurosis. It demanded of reality an illusory world, love, an absolute which it could never obtain, and thus destroyed itself by the dream.

—*Diary 1*, pg. 280

◆ 196 ◆

In the personal, there is more hope of learning why—*never* in history. In the personal there is some hope of truth—*never* in history. To confuse the Proustian *I* with narcissism is absurd. The *I* here is merely the eye of the microscope.

—*Joyous Transformation*, 1967

◆ 197 ◆

Laughter and tears are not separate experiences, with intervals of rest: they rush out together and it is like walking with a sword between your legs.

—House of Incest, pg. 31

◆ 198 ◆

Limitations, restrictions, defeats, come from within. I am fully responsible for my own restrictions.

—Diary 2, pg. 156

◆ 199 ◆

Loneliness increases as you ascend to more rarefied atmospheres.

—Diary 5, pg. 140

◆ 200 ◆

My attraction to drugs is based on an immense desire to annihilate awareness.

—Henry & June, pg. 207

◆ 201 ◆

We are much more severe judges of our own acts. We judge our
thoughts, our secret intents, our dreams even...

—*A Spy in the House of Love*, in *Cities of the Interior*, pg. 461

◆ 202 ◆

Life heals you if you allow it to flow, if you do not allow it to trap
you.

—*Diary 7*, pg. 232

◆ 203 ◆

It is undeniable that the source of all our miseries comes from our
obstinacy in maintaining that Paradise is a garden. The
psychoanalysts have added to the confusion by interpreting the
floating dreams as a flight into space. The mystic is the only one
who knows that all states of ecstasy are a state of floating in an
ambiance more heavy than air. I say, but do not repeat it to anyone
who is not ripe enough to receive it, Paradise is at the bottom of the
sea. And I can also prove to you that angels are ships. They have no
wings but large sails which they unfold noiselessly at night to cross
Eternity.

—*Diary 4*, pg. 7

My first vision of earth was water veiled. I am of the race of men and women who see all things through this curtain of sea, and my eyes are the color of water.

—*House of Incest*, pg. 15

Only from *within* can you influence, not by standing outside passing judgment.

—*Diary of Others*, 1957

Something always eludes the scientists, the poets, the stargazers, the biologists, the anthropologists. Something eludes the informers, detectives, police, lawyers. It is the dream. And what lies in the deformed mirrors of the dream and haunts our sleep is the secret of everything.

—*Diary 3*, pg. 251

One must not be afraid. One must know how to float as words do, without roots and without watering cans. One must know how to navigate without latitudes or longitudes and without motor. Without drugs and without burdens. One must learn to breathe like a wind-measuring instrument. The cord must be made of sand, the anchor of aurora borealis.

—*Diary 2*, pg. 128

◆ 208 ◆

We do not die individually, but in fragments with the deaths of those we love.

—Diary of Others, 1957

◆ 209 ◆

99 per cent of the world is an inert, unthinking mass, led by the nose, empty, blind, deaf and dumb, whom a few people manipulate. It's a rather sad picture.

—Diary of Others, 1964

◆ 210 ◆

Patients weep when they discover they are their own victimizers and not the victim of others. They weep when they discover they are responsible for their own suffering.

—Diary 2, pg. 26

◆ 211 ◆

Why must I change so? I do not feel anything. I am cold and do not understand religion at the moment, and I know, I understand that it is my exalted nature that causes its sudden coldness for what I used to adore and in which I put all the strength of my passion.

—Reunited, pg. 42

Consciousness

◆ 212 ◆

I do not respond to religious preoccupations. I'm a pagan. Religion comes from within us and is expressed by our humanity.

—Diary 7, pp. 285-286

◆ 213 ◆

She lacks the core of sureness, she craves admiration insatiably. She lives on reflections of herself in others' eyes. She does not dare to be herself.

—Henry & June, pg. 15

◆ 214 ◆

In order to be a mirror reflecting others, in order to relate to others, you have to be a person first of all.

—Conversations with Anaïs Nin, pg. 20

◆ 215 ◆

The mold we give to our lives is so that there will be no cataclysms. The order we seek we are willing to surrender to the flow of life at any time, but it is there as a brake on a car, and our health is a brake. We put brakes on, against our temperament.

—Diary 1, pg. 214

◆ 216 ◆

Just as the deep-sea diver carries a tank of oxygen, we have to carry
the kernel of our individual growth with us into the world in order
to withstand the pressures, the shattering pressures of outer
experiences.

—In Favor of the Sensitive Man, pg. 62

◆ 217 ◆

June and I were walking together over the dead leaves crackling
like paper. She was weeping over the end of a cycle. How one must
be thrust out of a finished cycle in life, and that leap the most
difficult to make—to part with one's faith, one's love, when one
would prefer to renew the faith and re-create the passion. The
struggle to emerge out of the past, clean of memories; the
inadequacy of our hearts to cut life into separate and final portions;
the pain of this constant ambivalence and interrelation of
emotions; the hunger for frontiers against which we might learn as
upon closed doors before we proceed forward; the struggle against
diffusion, new beginnings, against finality in acts without finality
or end, in our cursedly repercussive being.

—Diary 1, pp. 142-143

◆ 218 ◆

We should not bring to the collective an unfinished, distressed,
chaotic, confused, sick, or hurt self.

—In Favor of the Sensitive Man, pg. 63

◆ 219 ◆

The refusal to be angry is crippling.

—*Diary of Others*, 1957

◆ 220 ◆

The relationship we have with the dead is an entirely new one.
Some trait which interfered with communion, with the flow of
love, die with them… With death all these barbed wires, these
alarm signals, these interferences in reception waves disappear and
one hears the true self more distinctly.

—*Diary 7*, pg. 44

◆ 221 ◆

The world needs truth. No matter how painful. Because when
people bury the truth it festers.

—*Diary 5*, pg. 149

◆ 222 ◆

The white man has invented glasses which make objects too near
or too far, cameras, telescopes, spyglasses, objects which put glass
between living and vision. It is the image he seeks to possess, not
the texture, the living warmth, the human closeness.

—*Diary 5*, pg. 3

◆ 223 ◆

What is immortality? When the spirit has a voice in words or color or stone or garden, which is transferable. Those who had no voice? Those we never knew, who dissolved—does not even science say their voices are still in the air? Who knows what we are breathing from the past?

—Joyous Transformation, 1974

◆ 224 ◆

We are punctual, a stressed, marked characteristic. We need order around us, in the house, in the life, although we live by irresistible impulses, as if the order in the closets, in our papers, in our books, in our photographs, in our souvenirs, in our clothes could preserve us from chaos in our feelings, loves, in our work...but this, we admit, is the part of the war against a threatening fragility.

—Diary 1, pg. 207

◆ 225 ◆

There is a time when yielding is not conceding but acceptance of the other's existence and also of the motivation for what he does.

—A Woman Speaks, pg. 17

I was more concerned about aging at 30 and 40 than now at 70. Because I found that if you live deeply, remain emotionally alive, curious, explorative, open to change, to new experiences, aging recedes. It is not chronological, it is psychic. I was against the depressing acceptance of chronology by Simone de Beauvoir. Bow to age, she says. I say transcend it.

—Joyous Transformation, 1974

Being famous is destructive if taken as narcissistic appraisal but creative if taken as means of discovery and expansion. I discover *others* who come to me. More doors are opened. It is not a static pose to accept a tribe, but a means to explore and discover.

—Joyous Transformation, 1972

I believe liberation is never achieved by one segment of people; it has to be simultaneous and it has to happen to all of us.

—A Woman Speaks, pg. 35

◆ 229 ◆

If the whole world sought reality and truth, it would mean the end of war. To *remove* what makes you angry, or unjust, or aggressive, or unable to allow others to think and be different... And it can't be done from the outside. It is then you are ready to live for bigger aims, and better friendships.

—*Diary of Others*, 1955

◆ 230 ◆

What is the greatest need of human beings? What is it they seek from me always? Intimacy.

—*Diary 6*, pg. 86

◆ 231 ◆

When you give someone flavors of other worlds, you also give the poison of discontent.

—*Diary of Others*, 1955

What we call our destiny is truly our character and that character can be altered. The knowledge that we are responsible for our actions and attitudes does not need to be discouraging, because it also means that we are free to change this destiny. One is not in bondage to the past which has shaped our feelings, to race, inheritance, background. All this can be altered if we have the courage to examine how it formed us. We can alter the chemistry provided we have the courage to dissect the elements.

—Diary 1, pg. 126

The family is an artificial bondage. It is false and meaningless. Why do people continue to pay tribute to it...to feed its jaws, submit to its verdicts... In friendship there is sincerity, and selection.

—Diary of Others, 1955

Neurosis is a kind of unhealable wound. A man with an unhealable wound does not have much sympathy for others.

—Diary of Others, 1956

◆ 235 ◆

Women always think that when they have my shoes, my dress, my hairdresser, my make-up, it will all work the same way. They do not conceive of the witchcraft that is needed. They do not know that I am not beautiful but that I only appear to be at certain moments.

—Henry & June, pg. 188

◆ 236 ◆

The one thing I dislike in the knowledge of psychoanalysis is that once one has discovered one's fatality lies in one's own power, you suspect tragedies to be self-created, that there is danger of no longer believing in bad luck, but in one's own responsibility.

—Diary of Others, 1962

◆ 237 ◆

Let me think of death as the Balinese do, as a flight to another life, a joyous transformation, a release of our spirit so it might visit all other lives.

—Diary 7, pg. 336

WOMEN AND MEN

◆ 238 ◆

I have known men who make marvelous mothers; I have known men who do things which we consider feminine much better than women. I have known women who have extraordinary courage in action and no fear at all. I do think the virtues of in each of us are distributed, not necessarily in women or men.

—Conversations with Anaïs Nin, pg. 30

◆ 239 ◆

Not owed even to my father's love of beauty, but to his need of conquest is my mother's misery, the loss of a father I loved, the loss of a musical world, an art world, Europe, a crippled childhood, a violent transplantation to a country I hate, the loss of my languages Spanish and French, of my people, the loss of my confidence as a woman, my neurosis. So much due to what I believed was my father's interest in pretty women! No wonder…that a pretty woman is for me the announcement of catastrophe, a fire alarm, war, death, destruction.

—Trapeze, pg. 145

The child and the mother. Just keep saying he is a child, and she the mother, for thus are many men's acts covered and transfigured. The woman becomes the mother and then she can forgive anything. The child of course does not know when he is hurting the mother. He does not see when she is tired, he is baffled when she is ill and does nothing for her. The child is passive, yielding, demanding and giving nothing. If the mother weeps he will throw his arms around her. Then he will go and do again that which makes her weep. The child never thinks of the mother except as the all giver, the all forgiving, the indefatigable love.

—*Nearer the Moon*, pg. 272

◆ 241 ◆

When I break glasses in a night club, as the Russians do, when my unconscious breaks out in wild rebellions, it is against life which has crippled these idealistic, romantic men. I respect these men, cold, pure, faithful, devoted, moral, delicate, sensitive, and unequal to life, more than I respect the tough-minded ones who return three blows to one received, who kill those who hurt them.

—*Diary 1*, pg. 175

◆ 242 ◆

I believe in the couple, in two people, man and woman, or man and man, or woman and woman, who set out to find the balance between each other so as to meet the problems of life.

—*Conversations with Anaïs Nin*, pg. 50

Women and Men

◆ 243 ◆

Do not, I say to today's women, please do not mistake sensitivity for weakness. This was the mistake which almost doomed our culture. Violence was mistaken for power, the misuse of power for strength.

—*In Favor of the Sensitive Man*, pg. 54

◆ 244 ◆

A man who dominates is a man who does not love. He has a tremendous animal vitality, a force, which conquers. He conquers, people are subjected by him, but he neither loves nor understands.

—*A Literate Passion*, pg. 5

◆ 245 ◆

Assurance of discontinuity is an inspiration to men just as continuity is an inspiration to women.

—*Diary of Others*, 1961

◆ 246 ◆

The woman of the future, who is really being born today, will be a woman completely free of guilt for creating and for her self-development. She will be a woman in harmony with her own strength, not necessarily masculine, or eccentric, or something unnatural.

—*In Favor of the Sensitive Man*, pp. 17-18

◆ 247 ◆

I would like to see women more concerned with women's contributions than with this great battle of attacking the men… We should be very busy creating the pattern of the new woman, honoring her gifts, finding out who were the women painters, who were the woman historians, who were the women psychologists, that we could be interested in.

—*Conversations with Anaïs Nin*, pg. 33

◆ 248 ◆

Women tend to blame men for where they are when they should be spending at least an equal amount of energy looking inward to see how they got there.

—*Conversations with Anaïs Nin*, pg. 247

Women and Men

I have seen romanticism outlast the realistic. I have seen men forget the beautiful women they have possessed, forget the prostitutes, and remember the first woman they idolized, the woman they could never have. The woman who aroused them romantically holds them.

—Henry & June, pg. 54

I judge a man and his strength by his creation, by his life. There are also powerful artistic creations that are meant only to compensate for human impotence. These are the ones who have deceived me.

—Reunited, pg. 57

I didn't want a separation to come out of a quarrel—but that is how it happens. One suddenly discovers after ten years that one is fundamentally misunderstood, which means not loved, and there you are. I'm very definite about this however—and it is not anger which makes me do it but complete disillusion—and that can't be altered. Sooner or later you were going to be alone, for your efforts were never towards union but *towards aloneness.* The time has come.

—Mirages, pg. 117

I knew the kind of unfaithfulness women could forgive was not the kind of unfaithfulness my Father had been guilty of. I knew that he was not a man one could easily forgive, because he was cold-blooded. He was not the natural man, that is, the man who lies, drinks, makes love, cheats, steals, devours others because he is of the jungle where such acts are natural. Those are the men women would forgive because they are natural. Because if the lion eats the lamb it is not an act of cruelty, not a premeditated one. Women sense this, and they forgive the cannibal, the man who is not aware of his strength, of his cruelty, of his ferocity. But the man like my Father who is the very essence of artifice, whose pleasure was a deliberate, conscious quest, whose conquests were not even born of a natural hunger but vanity, the need to accumulate conquests just to prove his power, this kind of self-indulgent behavior accompanied by hypocrisy, the need to make believe he possessed all the virtues, this was not forgivable. The natural man does not deceive, he is honest and does not pretend to be an ideal being. My Father was always acting the ideal being.

—*Nearer the Moon*, pg. 271

◆ 253 ◆

A woman is not really a *critic* but a penetrator. She does not judge, she understands.

—*A Literate Passion*, pp. 31-32

◆ 254 ◆

There are in any relationship—man with man, woman with woman, or man with woman—tensions created by differences in temperament and vision. Creation consists of integrating these differences into an effective balance.

—*Conversations with Anaïs Nin*, pg. 73

◆ 255 ◆

A woman is jealous only when she has nothing, but I who am the most loved of all women, what can I be jealous of?

—*Hell Hath no Fury*, pg. 11

◆ 256 ◆

It is my secrecy which makes you unhappy, my evasions, my silences. And so I have found a solution. Whenever you get desperate with my mysteries, my ambiguities, here is a set of Chinese puzzle boxes. You have always said that I was myself a Chinese puzzle box. When you are in the mood and I baffle your love of confidences, your love of openness, your love of sharing experiences, then open one of the boxes. And in it you will find a story, a story about me and my life. Do you like this idea? Do you think it will help us to live together?

—*Collages*, pg. 29

He rolled over and fell asleep. No noise, no care, no work undone, no imperfection unmastered, no word unsaid ever kept him awake. He could roll over and forget. He could roll over with such a grand indifference and let everything wait. When he rolled over the day ended. Nothing would be carried over into the next day. The next day would be absolutely new and clean. He just rolled over and extinguished everything—work, books, talk, love, laughter, people, himself, the whole world. Just rolling over.

—*The Winter of Artifice*, Paris edition, pg. 28

No man or woman knows what will be born in the darkness of their intermingling; so much besides children, so many invisible births, exchanges of soul and character, blossoming of unknown selves, liberation of hidden treasures, buried fantasies...

—*The Four-Chambered Heart*, pg. 277

The most important thing is to obey the flow of life if you have it in you. Our growth is like that of plants; if they are not permitted to grow, they become stunted and twisted. It is not easy for the woman. Man usually fulfills all his desires, but woman has a need to protect and to preserve at the same time. I have known all the torments of guilt for expansion which seemed a threat to those I loved, yet I know that if those life impulses had been crippled, they would have turned into destructions. I needed constant absolution.

—*Diary of Others*, 1962

She was sewing together the little proofs of his devotion out of which to make a garment for her tattered love and faith. He cut into the faith with negligent scissors, and she mended and sewed and rewove and patched. He wasted, and threw away, and could not evaluate or preserve, or contain, or keep his treasures. Like his ever torn pockets, everything slipped through and was lost, as he lost gifts, mementos—all the objects from the past. She sewed his pockets that he might keep some of their days together, hold together the key to the house, to their room, to their bed. She sewed the sleeve so he could reach out his arm and hold her, when loneliness dissolved her. She sewed the lining so that the warmth would not seep out of their days together, the soft inner skin of their relationship.

—*Ladders to Fire*, in *Cities of the Interior*, pg. 46

◆ 261 ◆

He was jealous of her future, and she of his past.

—*Delta of Venus*, pg. 127

◆ 262 ◆

The women of Japan are at once the most present and the most elusive inhabitant of any country I have seen. They are everywhere, in restaurants, streets, shops, museums, subways, trains, fields, hotels and inns, and yet achieve a self-effacement that is striking to foreign women. In the hotels and inns they are solicitous, thoughtful, helpful to a degree never dreamed of except by men, but this care and tender lavishness is equally given to women visitors. It was as if one's dream of an ever-attentive, ever-protective mother were fulfilled on a collective scale, only the mother is forever young and daintily dressed. They were laborious and yet quiet, efficient and yet not intrusive or cumbersome.

—*Joyous Transformation*, 1966

◆ 263 ◆

The Japanese women expect to be liberated by marriage to an American. It does not liberate them. The American man demands a Japanese wife. Liberation comes from within.

—*Diary 7*, pg. 51

◆ 264 ◆

The beauty of a relationship based on a disparity of age is that youth abolishes the twilight and conceals and retards the reign of death.

—Diary of Others, 1956

◆ 265 ◆

The cape held within its folds something of what she imagined was a quality possessed exclusively by man: some dash, some audacity, some swagger of freedom denied to woman.

—A Spy in the House of Love, in *Cities of the Interior*, pg. 366

◆ 266 ◆

You speak of strength—but you see I'm not an oak—and that's what you need. You must find the life you really want, and the woman who can give it to you. For the first time I realize I am not the woman for you—you need an oak!

—Mirages, pg. 125

◆ 267 ◆

The helplessness engendered in woman by the married state and the man providing may be the ruin of her life.

—Joyous Transformation, 1974

◆ 268 ◆

I have shown young women that a woman can flower, create, love, and I have reduced their fear about aging.

—Joyous Transformation, 1974

◆ 269 ◆

The inner hatreds of men are now projected outside. There are fights in the streets. Revolutions in France, they say. Men did not seek to resolve their own personal revolutions, so now they act them out collectively.

—Diary 1, pg. 306

◆ 270 ◆

I never realized before, the *predominance* of men in all professions, nor did I realize fully the constant lowering of women's status. It is wonderful to see women struggling to get into filmmaking, into law, all professions. But I also find the radical feminists damaging, the men haters, the artificial lesbians, the vociferous, bitter, violent women who achieve nothing.

—Diary 7, pg. 283

There are a great many times we are passive in the face of destiny, forgetting that we really are able to be the captains of our destiny. We are taught a kind of passivity; the culture has taught us that a certain passivity is a feminine quality. So the day that I was told by Otto Rank that I was responsible for the failures, the defeats that had happened to me, and that it was in my power to conquer them, that day was a very exhilarating day. Because if you're told that you're responsible that means that you can do something about it. Whereas the people who say society is responsible, or some of the feminist women who say man is responsible, can only complain. You see if you put the blame on another, there is nothing *you* can do. I preferred to take the blame, because that also means that one can *act*, and it's such a relief from passivity, from being the victim.

—*A Woman Speaks*, pp. 48-49

◆ 272 ◆

To think of her in the middle of the day lifts me out of ordinary living.

—*Diary 1*, pg. 49

◆ 273 ◆

There is no mockery between women. One lies down at peace as on one's own breast.

—*House of Incest*, pg. 24

◆ 274 ◆

Today I said in the middle of the street to the passersby: "*No puedo mas*"—I wanted to shout it in Spanish—I don't know why: "*¡No puedo mas!* I can do no more." If you come back I know what awaits me: feeling your misery, your rebellion. I can't bear it. Because I'm a dreamer, I dreamed your dream of freeing you, but I didn't know that the human being breaks—and there you are. The human being broke. You dreamed impossible things and left me the work of fulfilling them. You escaped every constraint, every discipline, every slavery to love, to human life, every sacrifice. You're at peace with yourself. Well, that's an achievement.

—*Mirages*, pg. 126

◆ 275 ◆

Watch the conqueror well, watch the man or woman who dominates another: he is not the one who loves. The one who loves is the one who is dominated.

—*A Literate Passion*, pg. 5

◆ 276 ◆

I wished that in my next life I might be a lover of women. I have now known so many, so fascinating, so intelligent.

—*Joyous Transformation*, 1974

History is the story of man's thirst for power with its consequent inhumanity. The writing of women may indicate a new feminine direction...

A proper evaluation, a proper perspective and appreciation of women's writing may help to balance the unbalanced forces of the world today. If we have had an excess of violence, of crime and war, we may find in women's writing the persistent devotion to opposite concerns.

—The Mystic of Sex, pg. 87

In most casual love affairs the men and women withdraw from each other. They have no need to continue the embrace.

—Joyous Transformation, 1976

There is a resemblance between men and women, not a contrast. When a man begins to recognize his feeling, the two unite. When men *accept* the sensitive side of themselves, they come alive... We speak of the masculine and the feminine, but they are the wrong labels. It is really more a matter of poetry versus intellectualization.

—In Favor of the Sensitive Man, pg. 95

I do not want to be the leader. I refuse to be the leader. I want to
live darkly and richly in my femaleness. I want a man lying *over*
me, always *over* me. *His* will, *his* pleasure, *his* desire, *his* life, *his*
work, *his* sexuality the touchstone, the command, my pivot. I don't
mind working, holding my ground intellectually, artistically; but as
a woman, oh, God, as a woman I want to be dominated. I don't
mind being told to stand on my own feet, not to cling—all *that* I
am capable of doing—but I am going to be pursued, fucked,
possessed by the will of a male at *his* time, his bidding.

—*Incest*, pg. 57

Women and Men

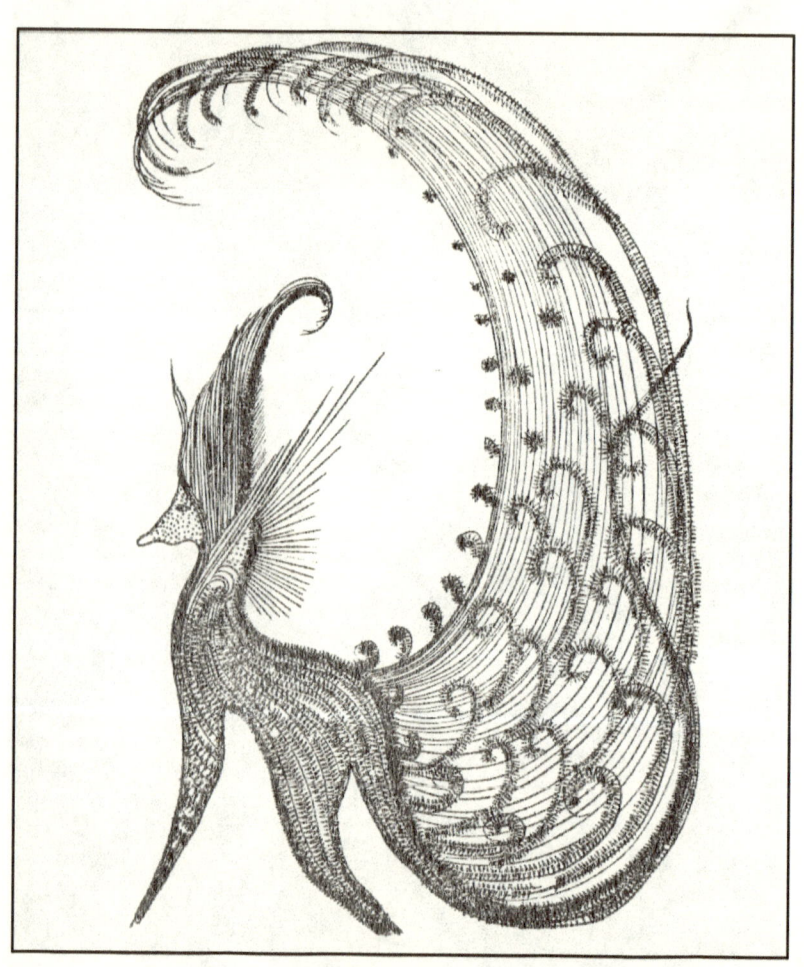

WRITING AND ART

・ 281 ・

I walked into my own book, seeking peace.

—House of Incest, pg. 62

・ 282 ・

Only when the poet and the scientist work in unison will we have living experiences and knowledge of the marvels of the universe as they are being discovered.

—Diary 7, pg. 70

・ 283 ・

There is a special kind of reward which is wonderful, and it's something which, I think, only artists enjoy. It has nothing to do with material rewards. It's the reward of finding your people, the chance to make a world, a population of your own, and that's wonderful because you find yourself as a connecting link between people who think as you do and feel as you do. And suddenly you're not alone.

—Conversations with Anaïs Nin, pg. 249

◆ 284 ◆

Some people read to confirm their own hopelessness. Others read to be rescued from it.

—*In Favor of the Sensitive Man*, pg. 64

◆ 285 ◆

I am the kind of woman no one imagines capable of writing, of doing all I have done, of handling a hot poker, of having a soul of her own.

—*Letters to Lawrence Durrell*, pg. 15

◆ 286 ◆

I am most awake to my Self as artist, as a solitary, unmated woman.

—*Incest*, pg. 329

◆ 287 ◆

I cannot tell the whole truth simply because I would have to write four journals at once.

—*Henry & June*, pg. 208

Writing and Art

What Americans read is the equivalent of *Reader's Digest,* prefabricated, preheated, prefrozen, predigested, prepared functional writing. Not the art of writing.

—Diary of Others, 1962

A big enough artist, I say, can eat anything, must eat everything and then alchemize it. Only the feeble writer is afraid of expansion.

—Diary 1, pg. 155

All creators are unhappy in life. All creators are absolutists.

—Fire, pp. 72-73

All my creation is an effort to weave a web of connection with the world; I am always weaving it because it was once broken.

—Diary 3, pg. 231

The only nonhuman existence is what we call our human life. If we live our human life and none other, directly, then we subject ourselves to the most inhuman of all conditions: slavery to family and national taboos, wars, illness, poverty, death. Even the phrase "earning our living" is inhuman. Without religion or art or analysis to transpose the stark horror, we fall into the malady of our age with its great devotion to naturalism. A painting in a house is there to represent a color, a form, a realm we may not have been able to possess. A book opens a realm which our need to earn a living may have made unattainable. Everything that helps us to transpose the unbearable into a myth also helps the creation of distance from our inhuman life, to allow us to mix a little objectivity with the harsh, violent torments of our human bondage.

—*Diary 5*, pg. 191

◆ 293 ◆

I am more interested in human beings than in writing, more interested in lovemaking than in writing, more interested in living than in writing. More interested in becoming a work of art than in creating one.

—*Diary 4*, pg. 177

◆ 294 ◆

Only in the fever of creation can I recreate my own lost life.

— The Winter of Artifice, Paris edition, pg. 118

◆ 295 ◆

I have always believed in André Breton's freedom, to write as one thinks, in the order and disorder in which one feels in thinks, to follow sensations and absurd correlations of events and images, to trust to the new realms they lead one into. "The cult of the marvelous." Also the cult of the unconscious leadership, the cult of mystery, the evasion of false logic. The cult of the unconscious as proclaimed by Rimbaud. It is not madness. It is an effort to transcend the rigidities and the patterns made by the rational mind.

—Diary 1, pg. 11

◆ 296 ◆

As an artist, America has killed me with insults, blindness, deafness, indifference. I can name all the offenders; that is the reality. They could not kill the life and beauty of my writing, but they could strangle the books.

— Trapeze, pg. 274

The necessity for fiction was probably born of the problem of taboo on certain revelations. It was not only a need of the imagination but an answer to the limitations placed on portrayal of others.

—The Novel of the Future, pg. 155

The musicians are playing the Schubert cello quintet—the long sweetness, tender accents, the wistful, lingering plaint and bursts of joy. Joy wins out. Every note is set dancing, starting gently, ending vigorously. Then the plaint again, the repetitions of the longing, the tenderness, the heartbeat and a burst of ecstasy. The lyrical tones mingle with soft shadowy secrets—feelings are suspended— then burst open, step step step toward intensity. Always a reverie, gentle and in unison, and then a tempestuous meeting of all the instruments. Peace, serenity, storm and undercurrent of intensity. The intensity wins in harmony and in moments of repose, reverie. The lullaby sets you dreaming; you float on tenderness, but a storm awakens you. Gently now, the violins, the viola, the cello lull you, repeating your most secret wish, lulling, caressing, swinging on a hammock of silk. Then the inner fires of the world burst and burn and spill over. All the reveries are forced to hide—one does not hear them anymore. Then the instruments seem to mourn the early reverie and seek it again. Drops of water from the trees, golden sparkle on the sea, words of passion, caressing notes, all light and sorrow.

—Diary 7, pg. 341

Writing and Art

◆ 299 ◆

My novels are not novels, they are surrealistic and allegorical.
Judged by all of America on a naturalistic Hemingway-ish basis,
naturally they failed.

—Joyous Transformation, 1966

◆ 300 ◆

The dream has to be translated into reality.

— The Novel of the Future, pg. 6

◆ 301 ◆

I don't like surrealism because it has no orientation, theme or core.
It is chaos.

—Letters to Lawrence Durrell, pg. 52

◆ 302 ◆

I gathered poets around me and we all wrote beautiful erotica. As
we were condemned to focus only on sensuality, we had violent
explosions of poetry. Writing erotica became a road to sainthood
rather than to debauchery.

—Diary 3, pg. 157

◆ 303 ◆

I find a danger in watching films. It is like passive dreaming. It requires no participation, no effort. It induces passivity. It is baby food; no need to masticate, no need to carve. There is no need to learn to play an instrument, to learn to read a book. People stretch on specially inclined chairs and receive the images in utter, infantile passivity. Speech, already inadequate in America, will soon disappear together with the ability to derive significance from the printed word. This is as radical a change as from monkey to man, it is an evolution from man into automaton.

—Diary 5, pg. 72

◆ 304 ◆

I have only been able to bear the cruelties and abominations of human life by transfigurations: art, poetry, fantasy.

— Trapeze, pg. 290

◆ 305 ◆

Now I have become the tigress. I will make men suffer. I will not suffer anymore. Suffer, suffer, suffer. I write my book then, observing everything. No wasted emotion. No neuroses. Art. Hardness. The impersonal! I want to write the vilest book on incest—stark, real.

—Incest, pp. 314-315

◆ 306 ◆

To capture the drama of the unconscious, one had to start with the key, and the key was the dream. But the novelist's task was to pursue this dream, to unravel its meaning; the goal was to reach the relation of dream to life; the suspense was in finding this which led to a deeper significance of our acts.

—*The Novel of the Future*, pg. 118

◆ 307 ◆

We do not escape into philosophy, psychology, and art—we go there to restore our shattered selves into whole ones.

—*In Favor of the Sensitive Man*, pg. 17

◆ 308 ◆

As Americans, we have a collective neurosis. My belief is that we create better without it. There are a great many romantic notions that neuroses are necessary; that pain and sorrows are necessary for the writer. I reject this as a false romanticism.

—*Conversations with Anaïs Nin*, pg. 239

◆ 309 ◆

I want to write only about what I love.

—*Diary of Others*, 1955

♦ 310 ♦

For the neurotic, the merging of the subconscious and the conscious may be risky, just as it is for the users of drugs. But for the writer who is aware of the way in which this connection exists in reality and nourishes creativity, the sooner he can achieve a synthesis among intellect, emotion, and instinct, the sooner his work will be integrated.

— *The Novel of the Future*, pg. 7

♦ 311 ♦

I sat at the typewriter, saying to myself: Write, you weakling; write, you madwoman, write your misery out, write out your guts, spill out what is choking you, shout obscenely.

—*Incest*, pg. 308

♦ 312 ♦

I stress the expansion and elaboration of language. In simplifying it, reducing it, we reduce the power of our expression and our power to communicate. Standardization, the use of worn-out formulas, impedes communication because it does not match the subtlety of our minds or emotions, the multimedia of our unconscious life.

— *The Novel of the Future*, pg. 93

◆ 313 ◆

I think now that at the root of all my writing lies the fact that very early in life I lost the desire to participate with others on the basis laid down by society. All I have been doing, possibly, in my work, is to protest and explain wherein I'm different.

—Diary 3, pg. 202

◆ 314 ◆

There have always been folk art and classical art. They cross-fertilize, but they should not be confused. America thinks all art can be folk art—and it cannot. They are succeeding in destroying art. And leadership. They will soon have masses of uneducated people.

—Diary of Others, 1956

◆ 315 ◆

I thought of my difficulties with writing, my struggles to articulate feelings not easily expressed. Of my struggles to find a language for intuition, feelings, instincts which are, in themselves, elusive, subtle, and wordless.

—Diary 1, pg. 276

◆ 316 ◆

Of what interest is the story of one woman? I say the story of one woman is no different than the story of a million women. I mean, one woman speaks, that's all. One talks or paints for the others who can't.

—*A Woman Speaks*, pg. 94

◆ 317 ◆

If you close doors, you close up the writing too. When the self is there, you can choose between an objective or a subjective work. It will be *you* in either case.

—*Joyous Transformation*, 1974

◆ 318 ◆

Immediate impressions have a life which memory cannot re-create.

—*Diary 7*, pg. 137

◆ 319 ◆

In chaos there is fertility.

—*Diary 1*, pg. 118

◆ 320 ◆

What we read intellectually doesn't change our life as much was what we absorb emotionally. So to experience writing emotionally, it has to have rhythm and color and all the things that appeal to the senses.

—Conversations with Anaïs Nin, pg. 129

◆ 321 ◆

It is terrible that a writer should depend on such a politically corrupt system as that of reviews.

—Diary 7, pg. 65

◆ 322 ◆

It took a life in hell and many lives of painful explorations, and it took even a dangerous sojourn in the world of madness and the capacity to return to tell what I have told.

—Diary 5, pg. 82

◆ 323 ◆

Love and music make of dissonant fragments a symphonic whole.

—Joyous Transformation, 1975

◆ 324 ◆

Music is fluid, emotions are fluid. We are not chronologically organized: sometimes we're living in the past, sometimes we're in the present, another day perhaps we're obsessed with the future. Our memory fades back and forth and is very fluid. So the closer we come to creating that feeling in our work, the closer we come to what life is, which is constant change and openness and evolution.

—*Conversations with Anaïs Nin*, pg. 130

◆ 325 ◆

Jazz is the music of the body. I wish I could give back to the jazz musicians the joys they have given me. I feel jazz in my blood, in my nerves, in my flesh. I receive the drumming right in my body.

—*Diary 5*, pg. 154

◆ 326 ◆

Music spilling out of from the eyes in place of tears, music spilling from the throat in place of words, music falling from his fingertips in place of caresses, music exchanged between us instead of love, yearning on five lines, the five lines of our thoughts, our reveries, our emotions, our unknown self, our giant self, our shadow.

—*The Winter of Artifice*, Paris edition, pg. 147

I let the freedom come first. I let myself write whatever I want; the craftsman comes afterward.

—*Conversations with Anaïs Nin*, pg. 159

Music: It is as if the strings strained away the dross. Sharp ends soften. Dreams float to the surface. Memories pulsate, each note is a color, each note is a voice, a new cell awakened. It stills other sounds, drowns the harsh ones, it erects spirals and new planets. When the heart acquires rough edges, there is the muting effect. When the heart freezes, music liquefies it. When it is lonely, secret notes will escape and find their way to the pulse, restore its universal rhythms. It is remote and gentle. It sobs for you. It laments, it rejoices, it explodes with vigor and life. It never allows our body to die because every wish, every fantasy breathes and moves as if we were in the place of our first birth, the ocean. The notes fly so much farther than words. There is no other way to reach the infinite.

—*Joyous Transformation*, 1975

The creative personality never remains fixed on the first world it discovers. It never resigns itself to anything. That is the deepest meaning of rebellion...

—*The Novel of the Future*, pg. 197

No rest for me anywhere. No rest from writing, awareness, insights, memories, fantasies, analogies, free associations. Writing becomes imperative for a surcharged head.

—Diary 5, pg. 48

Perhaps behind our occasional hostility toward the artist and writer there may be a slight tinge of jealousy. The man or woman who for the sake of family life, children, takes up work he does not like, disciplines himself, sacrifices some fantasy he had once, to travel or to paint, or even possibly to write, may feel toward the artist and writer a jealousy of his adventurous life. The artist and the writer have generally paid the full price for their independence and for the privilege of doing work they love, or for their artistic rebellions against standardized living or values.

—Diary 5, pg. 56

Poetry, I feel, can be allowed to cast a shadow far greater than the core which set it off, but abstractions, the dancing of the skeleton, if it becomes a dance of words, is dangerous.

—Letters to Lawrence Durrell, pg. 17

Writing and Art

I seem to be going deeper into writing as sensation—bathing in it uncritically as you do at a concert, seeking to be led only by the instinct, the pleasure in the flesh of words, the voluptuousness.

—*Letters to Lawrence Durrell*, pg. 51

◆ 334 ◆

Rebellions of all kinds attract to their activities weaklings who rebel because they cannot master, destroy because they cannot create.

—*Diary 2*, pg. 272

◆ 335 ◆

The important task of literature is to free man, not to censor him, and that is why Puritanism was the most destructive and evil force which ever oppressed people and their literature: it created hypocrisy, perversion, fears, sterility.

—*Diary 4*, pg. 66

◆ 336 ◆

I never generalize, intellectualize. *I see, I hear, I feel.* These are my primitive elements of discovery.

—*Diary 4*, pg. 153

◆ 337 ◆

I dream, I kiss, I have orgasms, I get exalted, I follow a gigantic creative plan, I compose, decompose, improvise, I write in my head, I listen to all, I hear all that is said…I am aware, I am everywhere…I am open to wounds, open to love, I am rooted to my devotions, I carry an obsessional current of storytelling, I am writing my own story but I am never separate, cut off—never blind, deaf, absent.

—*Nearer the Moon*, pg. 176

◆ 338 ◆

I did not go to the end with my father—an experience of destructtive hatred and antagonism. I created a reconciliation, and I am writing a novel of hatred.

—*Reunited*, pg. 142

◆ 339 ◆

I am helping women to live, to have courage, to feel, to believe in themselves.

—*Joyous Transformation*, 1974

◆ 340 ◆

The other night we talked about literature's elimination of the unessential, so that we are given a concentrated "dose" of life. I said, almost indignantly, "That's the danger of it, it prepares you to live, but at the same time, it exposes you to disappointments because it gives a heightened concept of living, it leaves out the dull or stagnant moments. You, in your books, also have a heightened rhythm, and a sequence of events so packed with excitement that I expected all your life to be delirious, intoxicated."

Literature is an exaggeration, a dramatization, and those who are nourished on it (as I was) are in great danger of trying to approximate an impossible rhythm. Trying to live up to Dostoevskian scenes every day. And between writers there is a straining after extravagance. We incite each other to jazz-up our rhythm.

—*Diary 1*, pg. 109

◆ 341 ◆

I was a mute child who needed to speak and who needed to write and who was lonely. Whatever the reasons were—and they were many and they're very complex—something made me concentrate on that craft which became vital to all of us, which was to write how we felt.

—*A Woman Speaks*, pg. 244

◆ 342 ◆

The writer is the duelist who never fights at the stated hour, who gathers up an insult, like another curious object, a collector's item, spreads it out on his desk later, and then engages in a duel with it verbally. Some people call it weakness. I call it postponement. What is weakness in the man becomes a quality in the writer. For he preserves, collects what will explode later in his work. That is why the writer is the loneliest man in the world; because he lives, fights, dies, is reborn always alone; all his roles are played behind a curtain. In life he is an incongruous figure.

—*Diary 1*, pg. 144

◆ 343 ◆

There are books which we read early in life, which sink into our consciousness and seem to disappear without leaving a trace. And then one day we find, in some summing-up of our life and our attitudes towards experience, that their influence has been enormous.

—*In Favor of the Sensitive Man*, pg. 57

◆ 344 ◆

When I heard the typewriter's dry crackling, I was happy.

—*The Winter of Artifice*, Paris edition, pg. 65

Writing and Art

I wrote for 20 years in a void, and I learned patience. So did Miller. Just keep writing.

—Joyous Transformation, 1971

So strange those hours of writing, so much like a spider web, but one in which people love to be caught and who start their own web of human connections.

—Diary 7, pg. 240

Proust's universality made his writing on music applicable to any music; his writing on jealousy fit jealousy at any time. He never fixed a date upon anything. A painting could apply to all painting. Very few novelists escaped the stamp of time so that the experience could only take place once.

—Joyous Transformation, 1976

◆ 348 ◆

Through books I discovered everything to be loved, explored, visited, communed with. I was enriched and given all the blueprints to a marvelous life, I was consoled in adversity, I was prepared for both joys and sorrows, I acquired one of the most precious sources of strength of all: an understanding of human beings, insight into their motivations.

—*Diary 7*, pg. 104

◆ 349 ◆

There was once a beautiful time when we could exchange a poem for a sack of potatoes. It is more complicated than that today, but it is still the same thing. I remember the fable of the swan who had been singing all summer while the ants worked, but who at the moment of finding himself destitute in the winter will find the ant and ask him to share some of the fruits of his work since the swan's songs had distracted and enchanted him during the summer.

—*Reunited*, pg. 107

◆ 350 ◆

What's so wonderful about the journal is that it helps you to make that inner journey and then finally to make a synthesis between all the parts of yourself, so that they become united.

—*A Woman Speaks*, pp. 164-165

Writing and Art

◆ 351 ◆

To say that the artist is not serving humanity is monstrous. He has been the eyes, the ears, the voice of humanity. He was always the transcendentalist who X-rayed our true states of being. His role in European culture is clear enough. Here he is given an inferior status, because he is not obviously and directly useful. His usefulness cannot be measured. The artist cannot serve directly.

—Diary 3, pg. 51

◆ 352 ◆

Put yourself right in the present. This was my principle when I wrote the diary—to write the thing I felt most strongly about that day. Start there and that starts the whole unraveling, because that has roots in the past and it has branches into the future.

—A Woman Speaks, pg. 163

◆ 353 ◆

The morning I got up to begin this book I coughed. Something was coming out of my throat: it was strangling me. I broke the thread which held it and yanked it out. I went back to bed and said: I have just spat out my heart.

—House of Incest, pg. 11

I remember that as children we were very unhappy because of great dissention between the parents. My father was a pianist and my mother was a singer. The quarrels would overwhelm and frighten us. But then suddenly there would be a quiet time. The piano would begin and my mother would begin to sing, and there would be peace again. And there would be great joy in the house, and the children felt free and they began to dance. This became for me a symbol and established a tremendous indebtedness and love for what I call the art spirits which we are celebrating today. That no matter what the human condition, no matter what kinds of infernos and destructive wars our dictators plunged us into, there was always this escape, this power to transfigure, transform, and transmute.

—*A Woman Speaks*, pg. 181

I believe there is no freedom in writing unless there is psychological freedom.

—*Joyous Transformation*, 1974

I call the artist the magician, because he holds the anti-toxins to cure us when we are shattered, or when we are in a state of despair or sorrow about what is happening outside.

—*A Woman Speaks*, pg. 185

◆ 357 ◆

D. H. Lawrence once said that the greatest problem of fiction was how to transport the living essence, the living quality of experience, into a prearranged art form. And in this dangerous transposition, this carrying of experience into fiction, the danger was that it would die in the process. Now in the diary no such death takes place because there is no distance. The living moment is caught. And in catching it, by accumulation and accretion, a personality emerges in all its ambivalences, contradictions and paradoxes, and finally, in its most living form.

—*Conversations with Anaïs Nin*, pp. 22-23

◆ 358 ◆

Each artist has to struggle to not conform to the culture but to add to the culture, to create the future.

—*A Woman Speaks*, pg. 193

◆ 359 ◆

This diary proves a tremendous, all engulfing craving for truth, since, to write it, I risk destroying the whole edifice of my illusions, all the gifts I made, all that I created and protected, everyone whom I saved from truth.

—*Diary 1*, pg. 242

◆ 360 ◆

I have run away with a part of my treasures, my memories, my obsession, with preserving, portraying, recording. All of us may die, but in these pages we will continue to smile, talk, make love.

—*Diary 3*, pg. 5

◆ 361 ◆

There are three different women who have the appearance of a woman, and who merge into one. The birth in the water, symbolism; then the inner life, imprisoned; then the delivery to the day. At night I paint solitary anxieties, dreams, which precede the real, human, healthy life. The depths of things. Our mysterious underwater life, which slips below what we are and do during the day.

—*Reunited*, pg. 205

◆ 362 ◆

I was creating a world which was an antithesis to the world around me which was full of sorrows, full of wars, full of difficulties. I was creating the world I wanted, and into this world, once it is created, you invite others and then you attract those who have affinities and this becomes a universe…

—*A Woman Speaks*, pg. 193

◆ 363 ◆

It is the cursed woman in me who causes the madness, the woman with her lover, her devotion, her shackles. Oh, to be free, to be masculine and purely artist. To care only about the art.

—*Incest*, pg. 308

◆ 364 ◆

At the core of my work was a journal written for the father I lost, loved and wanted to keep. I am personal. I am essentially human, not intellectual. I do not understand abstract act. Only art born of love, passion, pain.

—*Diary 1*, pg. 223

◆ 365 ◆

The result of the diary, for those who are really into it, is that they feel that I have helped make them aware of who they are, and where they are going, and how they want to get there.

—*Conversations with Anaïs Nin*, pg. 244

ABOUT THE AUTHOR: A CHRONOLOGY

1903 Anaïs Nin born in Neuilly, France

1913 Nin's father abandons family

1914 Nin, her mother and two brothers come to New York; begins her diary, in French

1920 Begins to write her diary in English

1923 Marries Hugh P. Guiler, a banker, in Cuba

1924 Nin and Guiler move to Paris; Nin continues her diary and dabbles in fiction

1931 Meets controversial American novelist Henry Miller in Louveciennes, France

1932 Becomes Miller's lover and is infatuated with his wife June; Edward Titus publishes Nin's *D. H. Lawrence: An Unprofessional Study*

1933 Reunites with her father and they begin an incestuous relationship

1934 Comes to New York to help Otto Rank psychoanalyze patients; becomes Rank's lover

1936 Self-publishes *The House of Incest* (Siana Editions)

1937 Meets Lawrence Durrell; she, Miller and Durrell begin planning a series of books

1939 Obelisk Press prints Nin's *The Winter of Artifice*; Nin and Guiler fly to New York to avoid oncoming war

1940 Reunites with her two lovers, Miller and Moré, in New York

1942 Self-publishes *Winter of Artifice* (Gemor Press); breaks with Miller

1944 Self-publishes *Under a Glass Bell* (Gemor Press)

1945 Self-publishes *This Hunger* (Gemor Press); meets Gore Vidal

1946 E. P. Dutton publishes *Ladders to Fire*

1947 Dutton publishes *Children of the Albatross*; Nin meets Rupert Pole and drives to California with him; begins her "double life," dividing her time between Pole in California and Guiler in New York; breaks with Moré

1950 Duell, Sloan and Pearce publishes *The Four-Chambered Heart*

1954 The British Book Centre publishes *A Spy in the House of Love*

1955 Nin bigamously marries Pole

1957 Avon republishes *A Spy in the House of Love*, which becomes Nin's best seller to date

1958 Self-publishes *Solar Barque*

1959 Self-publishes *Cities of the Interior*

1961 Signs with publisher Alan Swallow, who publishes *Seduction of the Minotaur* and reprints her earlier fiction

1964 Swallow publishes *Collages*, Nin's final work of fiction

1966 Harcourt Brace Jovanovich/Swallow publish volume one of *The Diary of Anaïs Nin*; Nin becomes famous and begins a popular lecture tour that would last for years

1967 Volume 2 of the *Diary* is published

1968 Swallow publishes *Novel of the Future*; Nin learns she has cancer

1969 Volume 3 of the *Diary* is published

1970 Nin is a popular lecturer at college campuses across the USA; she has radiation treatment for cancer

1971   Volume 4 of the *Diary* is published

1974   Volume 5 of the *Diary* is published; Nin learns she has a serious recurrence of cancer

1975   Nin's health deteriorates; remains in Los Angeles with Pole

1976   Volume 6 of the *Diary* is published; Nin is named Woman of the Year by the *Los Angeles Times*; cancer debilitates her in spite of many surgeries and treatments

1977   Nin dies of cancer at the age of 73; *Delta of Venus* is published posthumously and becomes her best seller

WORKS CITED

Auletris: Erotica. San Antonio: Sky Blue Press, 2016. Referenced as *Auletris*.

Cities of the Interior (*Ladders to Fire*, *Children of the Albatross*, *The Four-Chambered Heart*, *A Spy in the House of Love*, *Seduction of the Minotaur*). San Antonio: Sky Blue Press, 2013. Digital. Athens, OH: Swallow Press, 1974.

Collages. San Antonio: Sky Blue Press, 2010. Digital. Athens, OH: Swallow Press, 1964.

Delta of Venus: Erotica. New York: Harcourt Brace Jovanovich, 1977. Referenced as *Delta of Venus*.

The Diary of Anaïs Nin, Volume 1, 1931-1934. New York: Harcourt Brace Jovanovich, 1966. Referenced as *Diary 1*.

The Diary of Anaïs Nin, Volume 2, 1934-1939. New York: Harcourt Brace & World, Inc., 1967. Referenced as *Diary 2*.

The Diary of Anaïs Nin, Volume 3, 1939-1944. New York: Harcourt Brace Jovanovich, 1969. Referenced as *Diary 3*.

The Diary of Anaïs Nin, Volume 4, 1944-1947. New York: Harcourt Brace Jovanovich, 1971. Referenced as *Diary 4*.

The Diary of Anaïs Nin, Volume 5, 1947-1955. New York: Harcourt Brace Jovanovich, 1974. Referenced as *Diary 5*.

The Diary of Anaïs Nin, Volume 6, 1955-1966. New York: Harcourt Brace Jovanovich. 1976. Print. Digital. Referenced as *Diary 6*.

The Diary of Anaïs Nin, Volume 7, 1966-1974. New York: Harcourt Brace Jovanovich, 1980. Referenced as *Diary 7*.

The Diary of Others: The Unexpurgated Diary of Anaïs Nin, 1955-1966, forthcoming. Referenced as *Diary of Others*.

The Early Diary of Anaïs Nin, Volume 2, 1920-1923. New York: Harcourt Brace Jovanovich, 1982. Referenced as *Early Diary 2*.

The Early Diary of Anaïs Nin, Volume 3, 1923-1927. New York: Harcourt Brace Jovanovich, 1983. Referenced as *Early Diary 3*.

The Early Diary of Anaïs Nin, Volume 4, 1927-1931. New York: Harcourt Brace Jovanovich, 1985. References as *Early Diary 4*.

Fire: From "A Journal of Love," The Unexpurgated Diary of Anaïs Nin, 1933-1937. New York: Harcourt Brace, 1995. Referenced as *Fire*.

Henry and June: From the Unexpurgated Diary of Anaïs Nin. New York: Harcourt Brace Jovanovich, 1986. Referenced as *Henry & June*.

Hell Hath No Fury: Women's Letters from the End of the Affair. New York: Carroll & Graf, 2002. Referenced as *Hell Hath no Fury*.

House of Incest. San Antonio: Sky Blue Press, 2010. Digital. Athens, OH: Swallow Press, 1995.

In Favor of the Sensitive Man and Other Essays. New York: Harcourt Brace Jovanovich, 1976. Referenced as *In Favor of the Sensitive Man*.

Incest: From "A Journal of Love," The Unexpurgated Diary of Anaïs Nin, 1932-1933. New York: Harcourt Brace Jovanovich, 1992. Referenced as *Incest*.

A Joyous Transformation: The Unexpurgated Diary of Anaïs Nin, 1966-1977, forthcoming. Referenced as *Joyous Transformation*.

Letters to Lawrence Durrell, 1937-1977. Germantown: Sky Blue Press, 2020. Referenced as *Letters to Lawrence Durrell.*

Little Birds: Erotica. New York: Harcourt Brace Jovanovich, 1979.

Mirages: The Unexpurgated Diary of Anaïs Nin, 1939-1947. San Antonio: Sky Blue Press, 2013. Digital. Athens, OH: Swallow Press/Sky Blue Press, 2013. Print. Referenced as *Mirages.*

The Mystic of Sex. Santa Barbara: Capra Press, 1995.

Nearer the Moon: The Unexpurgated Diary of Anaïs Nin, 1937-1939. New York: Harcourt Brace, 1996. Referenced as *Nearer the Moon.*

The Novel of the Future. San Antonio: Sky Blue Press, 2014. Digital. Athens, OH: Swallow Press, 1968.

Trapeze: The Unexpurgated Diary of Anaïs Nin, 1947-1955. San Antonio: Sky Blue Press, 2017. Athens, OH: Swallow Press/Sky Blue Press, 2017. Print. Referenced as *Trapeze.*

Under a Glass Bell. San Antonio: Sky Blue Press, 2010. Digital. Athens, OH: Swallow Press, 2014.

The Winter of Artifice (Paris edition). Troy, MI: Sky Blue Press, 2007.

A Woman Speaks. Sky Blue Press (digital publication pending). Athens, OH: Swallow Press, 1975.

PERMISSIONS INFORMATION

Note: Quotations from *Conversations with Anaïs Nin* are cited as below:

Quotation numbers 145, 152, 248, 283, 308, and 365 originally appeared in *The New Orleans Review*, vol. 5, no. 2.

Quotation numbers 163, 238, and 247 were originally transcribed from Pacifica Radio Archives.

Quotation numbers 320 and 324 originally appeared in *New Woman*, 17 December, 1971.

Quotation number 2 originally appeared in *Helicon Nine Journal of Women's Arts and Letters*, vol. 1, no. 1.

Quotation number 254 originally appeared in *Ramparts Magazine*, May 1971.

Quotation number 327 originally aired in 1972 on WFMT-FM in Chicago.

ALSO AVAILABLE FROM SKY BLUE PRESS

ANAIS: An International Journal Anthology, 1983-2001 (print, ebook)

Letters to Lawrence Durrell, 1937-1977 by Anaïs Nin (print, ebook)

Reunited: The Correspondence of Anaïs and Joaquín Nin 1933-1940 by Anaïs Nin and Joaquín Nin (print, ebook)

Auletris: Erotica by Anaïs Nin (print, ebook, audiobook)

Trapeze: The Unexpurgated Diary of Anaïs Nin, 1947-1955 by Anaïs Nin (print, ebook)

Mirages: The Unexpurgated Diary of Anaïs Nin, 1939-1947 by Anaïs Nin (print, ebook)

The Portable Anaïs Nin by Anaïs Nin, ed. Benjamin Franklin V (print, ebook)

D.H. Lawrence: An Unprofessional Study by Anaïs Nin (ebook)

House of Incest by Anaïs Nin (ebook)

The Winter of Artifice: 1939 Paris Edition by Anaïs Nin (print, ebook)

Under a Glass Bell by Anaïs Nin (ebook)

Stella by Anaïs Nin (ebook)

Ladders to Fire by Anaïs Nin (ebook)

Children of the Albatross by Anaïs Nin (ebook)

The Four-Chambered Heart by Anaïs Nin (ebook)

A Spy in the House of Love by Anaïs Nin (ebook)

Seduction of the Minotaur by Anaïs Nin (ebook)

Cities of the Interior by Anaïs Nin (ebook)

Collages by Anaïs Nin (ebook)

The Novel of the Future by Anaïs Nin (ebook)

Anaïs Nin: The Last Days, a Memoir by Barbara Kraft (ebook)

Anaïs Nin's Lost World: Paris in Words and Pictures 1924-1939 by Britt Arenander (print, ebook)

Anaïs Nin Character Dictionary and Index to Diary Excerpts by Benjamin Franklin V (print, ebook)

A Café in Space: The Anaïs Nin Literary Journal, Vol. 1 by Anaïs Nin, Janet Fitch, Lynette Felber... (print, ebook)

A Café in Space: The Anaïs Nin Literary Journal, Vol. 2 by Anaïs Nin, Benjamin Franklin V, Masako Meio... (print, ebook)

A Café in Space: The Anaïs Nin Literary Journal, Vol. 3 by Anaïs Nin, Gunther Stuhlmann, Richard Pine, James Clawson... (print, ebook)

A Café in Space: The Anaïs Nin Literary Journal, Vol. 4 by Anaïs Nin, Alan Swallow, John Ferrone, Yuko Yaguchi... (print, ebook)

A Café in Space: The Anaïs Nin Literary Journal, Vol. 5 by Anaïs Nin, Duane Schneider, Sarah Burghauser... (print, ebook)

A Café in Space: The Anaïs Nin Literary Journal, Vol. 6 by Anaïs Nin, Joaquín Nin y Castellanos, Tristine Rainer, Christie Logan... (print, ebook)

A Café in Space: The Anaïs Nin Literary Journal, Vol. 7 by Anaïs Nin, John Ferrone, Kim Krizan, Tristine Rainer... (print, ebook)

A Café in Space: The Anaïs Nin Literary Journal, Vol. 8 by Anaïs Nin, Benjamin Franklin V, Anita Jarczok, Kim Krizan... (print, ebook)

A Café in Space: The Anaïs Nin Literary Journal, Vol. 9 by Anaïs Nin, Anita Jarczok, Joel Enos... (print, ebook)

A Café in Space: The Anaïs Nin Literary Journal, Vol. 10 by Anaïs Nin, Benjamin Franklin V, Kim Krizan, William Claire, Erin Dunbar... (print, ebook)

A Café in Space: The Anaïs Nin Literary Journal, Vol. 11 by Anaïs Nin, Henry Miller, Alfred Perlès, John Tytell... (print, ebook)

A Café in Space: The Anaïs Nin Literary Journal, Vol. 12 by Anaïs Nin, Kim Krizan, Benjamin Franklin V... (print, ebook)

A Café in Space: The Anaïs Nin Literary Journal, Vol. 13 by Anaïs Nin, Barbara Kraft, Danica Davidson... (print, ebook)

A Café in Space: The Anaïs Nin Literary Journal, Vol. 14 by Anaïs Nin, Jessica Gilbey, Joaquín Nin-Culmell... (print, ebook)

A Café in Space: The Anaïs Nin Literary Journal, Vol. 15 by Anaïs Nin, Rupert Pole, Steven Reigns... (print, ebook)

A Café in Space: The Anaïs Nin Literary Journal, Anthology 2003-2018 (print, ebook)

Forthcoming:

The Diary of Others: The Unexpurgated Diary of Anaïs Nin, 1955-1966

A Joyous Transformation: The Unexpurgated Diary of Anaïs Nin, 1966-1977

A SELECTED LIST OF IN-PRINT WORKS
BY ANAÏS NIN

House of Incest—Swallow/Ohio University (OU) Press

The Winter of Artifice (1939 Paris edition)—Sky Blue Press

Under a Glass Bell—Swallow/OU Press

Cities of the Interior (consisting of 5 novels)—Swallow/OU Press
  Ladders to Fire
  Children of the Albatross
  The Four-Chambered Heart
  A Spy in the House of Love
  Seduction of the Minotaur

Collages—Swallow/OU Press

The Novel of the Future—Swallow/OU Press

The Diary of Anais Nin (7 volumes)—Houghton Mifflin Harcourt (HMH)

Unexpurgated diaries
  Henry & June—HMH
  Incest—HMH
  Fire—HMH
  Nearer the Moon—HMH
  Mirages—Sky Blue Press/Swallow/OU Press
  Trapeze—Sky Blue Press/Swallow/OU Press

Reunited: The Correspondence of Anaïs and Joaquín Nin, 1933-1940—Sky Blue Press/Swallow/OUP

Letters to Lawrence Durrell 1937-1977—Sky Blue Press

Erotica
  Delta of Venus—HMH
  Little Birds—HMH
  Auletris—Sky Blue Press

A SELECTED LIST OF WORKS
ABOUT ANAÏS NIN

ANAIS: An International Journal, ed. Gunther Stuhlmann
—Anaïs Nin Foundation

ANAIS: An International Journal Anthology, 1983-2001
—Sky Blue Press

A Café in Space: The Anaïs Nin Literary Journal, ed. Paul Herron
—Sky Blue Press

Barbara Kraft, *Anaïs Nin: The Last Days*—Sky Blue Press

Benjamin Franklin V, *Anaïs Nin Character Dictionary and Index to Diary Excerpts*—Sky Blue Press

Recollections of Anaïs Nin by her Contemporaries, ed.
Benjamin Franklin V—Ohio University (OU) Press

Anita Jarczok, *Writing an Icon: Celebrity Culture and the Invention of Anaïs Nin*—Swallow/OU Press

Anaïs Nin Blog
http://anaisninblog.skybluepresscom

Anaïs Nin Podcast
https://www.buzzsprout.com/1673362

Sky Blue Press on Facebook
https://www.facebook.com/skybluepress

Anaïs Nin on Twitter
@anaisninblog

www.ingramcontent.com/pod-product-compliance
Lightning Source LLC
Chambersburg PA
CBHW051924240626
47153CB00004B/1358